DESTINED TO DIE

Jim Gallery was no saint but he had never killed a man without good cause. Now, though, it looked as if it was his turn to die. Dawson, Kerle and Crane had promised themselves that Jim would die a lingering, horrifying death. He had been thrown into a well which was slowly filling up with water. Miraculously, Jim escaped, though he still had three vicious killers on his trail. Did he have the courage and the gun skills to plant the varmints on Boot Hill? Could he live long enough?

NORMAN LAZENBY

DESTINED TO DIE

Complete and Unabridged

LINFORD
Leicester

First hardcover edition published in Great Britain
in 2002 by Robert Hale Limited, London

Originally published in paperback as
'Gun Brat' by Wes Yancey

First Linford Edition
published 2004
by arrangement with
Robert Hale Limited, London

British Library CIP Data

Lazenby, Norman A. (Norman Austin)
Destined to die.—Large print ed.—
Linford western library
1. Western stories
2. Large type books
I. Title II. Yancey, Wes. Gun brat
813.5'2 [F]

ISBN 1–84395–130–4

Published by
F. A. Thorpe (Publishing)
Anstey, Leicestershire

Set by Words & Graphics Ltd.
Anstey, Leicestershire
Printed and bound in Great Britain by
T. J. International Ltd., Padstow, Cornwall
This book is printed on acid-free paper

1

Caught

Way up in the San Juan Mountains, some forty arid miles out of Delta, they were sure they had him cornered at last, and in the grimmest possible way. They had chased him right into this south-west corner of Colorado, avoiding towns where they were known to the sheriff.

Jim Gallery had been bone-tired and weary when they'd crept up on him. He thought he'd made no mistakes. He'd picked the rockiest way through the yellow canyons; he hadn't made a fire that night. Still, they'd crept up on him. The one mistake he had made was to get too damned tired.

Head on the ground, with only a blanket between him and the sand, his fatigued brain had heard the sound of scuffing boots a few dazed seconds too late. And then they'd been on him. Three of the hardest ruffians this side of hell. A boot in his ribs had been the first hint of grief. They stood over him — tall, lean, unshaven, dirty *hombres*, packing sixguns that looked like small cannons. They had plenty of reason for hating his guts.

Blue-eyed, blubbery-faced Kid Dawson hated him because he had killed his brother — in a fair fight most men had agreed.

And Max Kerle hated him because of money — the loot from the Drago Cattlemen's Bank, which had unaccountably been lost and had stayed lost according to Jim Gallery. Max Kerle was a gangling, hawk-like man who was wanted for robbery and murder right through Colorado and Wyoming.

And lastly, Stephen Crane, the older man, six feet of hard bone and stringy flesh, the man who still retained a cultured English accent along with an inhuman pleasure in cruelty of any kind. Flecks of grey in his hair and moustache gave him some dignity — but it was a disguise, for his soul was evil.

Jim Gallery rolled between their dusty boots as they kicked out in instant revenge for the arduous ride he had forced on them. Jim Gallery jerked like a creature seeking escape. He knew damned well there wasn't any, but he reacted like coiled steel to the kicks, trying to avoid them. They landed. A boot in his gut sickened him; another to the head dazed him, and a kick in the ribs went like a knife wound through his tired body.

All the time, in spite of being dazed and in pain, he tried to jerk away.

They had taken his gun a moment before alarm signals went off in his head, so there was no hope of a shoot-out. His horse and rifle were some distance away, stashed in the rocky cleft.

They kicked at him until blood spurted from his nose and face. They kicked until his ribs ached. Twice they had hit him in the crotch and he felt his senses swimming into a lousy world of pain. He sprawled, almost out to it, only his unbeatable sense of survival keeping him in a conscious state. He would fight until he died. It was pretty sure now that he would die. Right here in this goddamn arid land.

He had ridden into the badlands for the express purpose of losing his pursuers. He would have much preferred to have stayed in Delta — or Salida — drinking and complimenting the women, but he had had to ride out when he heard that Kid Dawson, Max Kerle and Stephen Crane were on his trail. He'd ridden out only a day ahead of the unholy trio. Seemed it had all been a lot of hard riding for nothing.

'We don't want to kill him. Not yet, my friends . . . perhaps we can think of a slower death for him than the merciful bullet . . . '

'He gun-marched you to that blamed sheriff in Alamosa — for the bounty,

4

Crane!' Kid Dawson blazed. 'You hate his guts for that . . .'

'It was a neat trick I won't forget,' admitted Stephen Crane. 'But that jail couldn't hold me. I was in worse holes in India . . . many years ago . . .'

'When you was an officer and a gentleman in the goddamn English army,' sneered Max Kerle. 'Yeah, we heard about it . . . you done told us plenty of times . . .'

'British army, you lanky ruffian,' corrected Stephen Crane gently.

'And you got chucked out!' went on Max Kerle. 'You ain't so good at explainin' just how that come about — but what the hell! What now? We got Gallery . . . do we kill him or not?'

Kid Dawson looked at the darkening sky. A moon began to show behind some clouds, and there was a rising wind. 'I figure there's a storm blowin' up. And them blamed horses are tuckered out. We could kill him — and then get set for the night.'

'You lack finesse, young man,' said

Stephen Crane. 'This devil killed your brother and all you can conjure up in the way of revenge is a quick bullet. Oh, no — he lives — at least until tomorrow — in some suspense — and then he should die in agony. Now in India, they have many exquisite ways of destroying a man . . .'

'Sure — we got Injuns here who can cook up the tortures of the damned,' snapped Max Kerle. 'But we ain't takin' a week over killin' this skunk. I want out of this blasted territory.'

'Are you sure he really doesn't know where the money from the Drago bank is stashed?' asked Stephen Crane.

'There was me, Gallery and Al Aston on that bank job,' said Max Kerle. 'Aston had to ride out like all hell with the dinero, while me and Gallery fooled the possemen with false trails. We kicked up some miles between us along that Laramie range — in and out of them damned hills which we knew like the backs of our hands. Then we high-tailed it to meet Aston with some

6

new horses we'd bought — didn't want to steal horseflesh that could've brought more law after us. When we finally hit the place where we had figured to find Aston — '

'He was there — dead!' supplied Stephen Crane impatiently. 'Yes, you've told us this tale many times. He was dead and the bank loot was nowhere in sight. You and Gallery searched for hiding places — looked for tracks of the killer — '

'Hoofmarks leadin' to the river,' grunted Max Kerle. 'The skunk must've ridden up or down the river for miles. We never cut sign of him again. A real smart *hombre* — whoever he was!'

Stephen Crane smiled and revealed teeth which were perfectly white, unusual for a man of his age in this frontier world. 'But you got around to thinking that somehow Gallery had pulled this trick. Because only you and Gallery knew that Al Aston would be hiding up in the hills near the river.

Gallery could have had an accomplice . . . '

Max Kerle glared down at Jim Gallery as he rested warily on the ground, ready to jerk into action if he got half a chance, or to twist to avoid another kick. Blood smeared his face. He made gurgling sounds in his nose and throat. He knew that already bruises were forming on his back and other parts of his body.

'He said it was some blasted stranger that robbed Al Aston,' snarled Max Kerle. 'I dunno . . . '

'Gallery never spent the money — that we do know. He didn't live high, wide and handsome,' mused Stephen Crane. 'I think, my lanky segundo, that there is some element of doubt — '

'All that damned dinero!' The other man went into one of his quick rages. 'Twenty thousand dollars . . . biggest thing I ever pulled . . . '

'You, Gallery and the late unlamented Al Aston,' corrected the other man. 'Yes, a neat little mystery which I admit intrigues me.' He looked down thoughtfully at the man crouching at their feet. 'You could try persuading Gallery to tell the truth now, Kerle.'

The gangling, hawk-faced man looked at the prisoner with some deep bitterness mixed with a grudging respect. 'He'd never tell me anythin' but the tale as it stands . . .

Kid Dawson glanced at the dark sky once more. 'Sure is a storm a-comin' up. I reckon we should find some place to shelter. Might rain. I seen these signs afore . . . '

'Ain't had rain for two months,' said Max Kerle.

'Waal, when' it rains in this territory, it sure makes a helluva splash. I seen these electrical storms afore.'

'Aw, there's a wind. Could blow miles away. Sure, it could rain — twenty miles back in the mountains! You never can tell.'

'Tell him, Steve!' shrilled the younger man. 'Tell him we need some place to shelter . . . '

The greying head jerked angrily. 'I've told you to call me Crane! I am not Steve to you! I was never Steve to anyone! Some years ago you'd have called me 'sir'! And damned well stood to attention!'

'Now ain't that mighty fine!' Max Kerle laughed coarsely and watched Kid Dawson and Stephen Crane with enjoyment. He always liked these exchanges, where the older man tried to exercise some authority, because, inwardly, he hated Crane's cuts. If the man had dropped down dead, he'd have laughed and turned him over with a boot. Crane meant nothing to him. He was a riding partner and crooked, which meant he knew some tricks for making quick money.

'Oh — all right — Crane!' Kid Dawson slurred the reply. 'You get real mean at times — Crane — '

'Call him 'sir'!' jeered Max Kerle. 'And maybe you should learn to salute, huh?'

'I ain't never been in no army,'

growled Kid Dawson. He stood with his legs apart, the stance of a gunny, with his hands unconsciously at hip height. One time Kid Dawson had packed twin Colts — until he realized they attracted unwelcome attention from other gun-happy characters — and he still had the habit of reaching for two guns. His blue eyes and curly fair hair had earned him the title of 'Kid' but he was about twenty-four. Now, dust-laden, smelling of horseflesh and stale sweat, he looked like the others — range-weary *hombres* who needed rest. 'I just figure we need some place to camp the night . . . '

Stephen Crane could always infuse cold authority into his even voice. 'Perhaps you're right, Dawson. It may rain. Well, I noticed a cave on the way up to this spot. We'll go there — and take our prisoner with us for further punishment.'

Max Kerle grinned sardonically, rubbing a hard, long-fingered hand over the week-old stubble on his chin. Kid

Dawson nodded, his fleshy, round face satisfied. The men turned for their horses, and at that moment Jim Gallery uncoiled like a scared antelope.

He had figured a split-second chance was better than none at all. A man could get lost in the surrounding darkness in no time.

But Max Kerle had reactions to match his hawk-like features and he dived in the same second that Jim Gallery struck for freedom. The two men collided. The thud could be heard distinctly.

And then they were fighting — one man with desperate urgency and the other with vicious enjoyment. Jim Gallery stood little chance because of the punishment he had already taken and Max Kerle knew that. He was able to sink a right and left fist into a weakened man. He felt Jim Gallery sag. He hit him again, a body blow, as if the man was a punch-bag. Jim Gallery rolled back to the earth.

'Hell, you ain't so tough, Gallery!

Figured you were rock at one time! Maybe you've gone soft . . . '

'Put a loop around his neck,' ordered Stephen Crane. 'Let's get mounted — and find his horse. We'll ride down to that cave. I must confess I suddenly feel the need for food and rest.'

A sneer curved the whiskered lips of Max Kerle but he said nothing. One thing he knew for sure; he was mighty tired of the other's fancy talk. He figured he didn't like Englishmen; a ranny in the West should use the local lingo. Well, they'd found Gallery and maybe that would be the end of riding with Stephen Crane — unless there was some money to be earned! In which case he might go along with him.

The cave was large and dry and they could hear running water not far away. At the moment their canteens held sufficient; still, the cave seemed a good spot. There was a grassy little nook which would take the horses for the night. Flat slabs of rock, weathered by unknown years of wind, rain and sandstorm, lay in front of the cave. In the faint light from the cloud-obscured moon, Stephen Crane found a curious hole in the rocky ground about a hundred yards from the cave mouth. It was almost like a well — a shaft. It had smooth sides and was about two yards in diameter and went down for about twenty feet.

He studied it for some moments and a cruel smile twisted his moustached lip. He went back to the others, and surveyed Jim Gallery.

'I've found a neat little cell for you, my man. Not an iron bar in sight — but better than that insalubrious hole into which you had me marched! Better because you will be unable to climb out. Even a lizard couldn't get out of that well . . . '

He was so enthusiastic about his find that he got the other two men to push Jim Gallery along to the smooth, round, rocky hole in the ground. They looked down and agreed that even a sidewinder could not climb out of the well. Then they grabbed Jim Gallery, shoved him to the edge of the hole and dropped him into the smooth, circular shaft.

Jim hit the bottom of the well with a thud that made his guts jerk. He lay dazed. When he stirred again his first thought was that no bones were broken because he could move without extreme agony. Still, he suffered physically. He had been knocked around and then slid into this well. He was bruised and hurt. His pants were torn and skin was scraped from his knees. Blood thickened on his face, clinging to his beard stubble. He was in bad shape.

He sat up, scowling fiercely and looking around. Then he got to his feet and moved around, hands splaying over the smooth walls of the well. It was a curious place, part natural and part man-made, he figured. Maybe some cave-dwelling Indians had fashioned the well, and it could be a hundred years old. But those thoughts did not matter a damn now! How could he get out?

He tried bracing himself against the wall and ramming his boots on the other side, but even with his six feet of length it was impossible to get much leverage. He tried it, with his hands hard against one side of the smooth perimeter and his feet braced hard against the other side. It was a muscle-wracking effort that got him about six feet from the bottom of the well and then he could not maintain the strain any longer. He dropped back, boots scuffing the loose chippings at the bottom of the well.

Well, he had been outsmarted! They'd got him. Three men with good reason to hate his guts. Max Kerle and his reaction to the missing loot! Kid Dawson who wore his resentment about his dead brother as if it was a religion! And Stephen Crane who felt evilly disposed to a man who had attempted to use him and his reputation for bounty money! Sure, they had good cause to hate him!

Jim Gallery stared at the distant

circle of sky. He saw the thick black clouds move ominously across the sky. Kid Dawson was right about the oncoming storm but maybe it would be highly localised and miss this area.

He glared again at the round patch of sky. He picked up a stone and tried to gouge a foothold in the wall of the well. The stone was soft and useless and he threw it away in disgust. He searched around for something harder, but there was nothing. They had taken his gun and knife. He had nothing. Anyway, it was an impossible task. And if they allowed him to live — or die — in this well, the sun would bake him into some state of exhaustion in no time.

Maybe this was the end of the trail for Jim Gallery. Well, he'd had a good time — not all of it morally credit-worthy, he supposed. He'd been a bad'un — but, maybe, not all bad. He had tried to do some good things along the way. He'd helped with a wagon train; nursed another man to health; even helped Indian women and kids.

And there had been Molly Peterson. She had been the one person he should have stayed with, but the wanderlust had beckoned. Molly! Maybe she was still in Denver, looking back at the shadow of the mountains and wondering if he would ride back one day.

Jim Gallery sat down, crouched, his head between his knees, nursing his aches and pains and waiting, his mind filled with many regretful thoughts.

In the nearby cave the three men stretched out, blankets under them, and stared at the fire at the cave mouth. They had hot coffee and a cooked slab of sidemeat from which they sliced chunks. They had hard tack and some three-day-old buns.

And then they heard the storm break. A flash of lightning cut the night sky and thunder rolled. The rain came a moment later, a lashing deluge that spat at the parched earth as if in a frenzy.

2

Escape

They listened to the pouring rain for a long time, secure in the cave, the fire just out of reach of the water and now a comforting mass of red embers. Kid Dawson kept saying, 'Sure, I was right. Real old downpour! Knew it would hit this area . . . '

'You don't know nothin'!' sneered Max Kerle. 'You're just makin' with the mouth, boy! Now shuddup!'

'That hellion out there will get mighty wet!' Kid Dawson said. He laughed. 'Real cold and wet . . . '

'That's just too bad — for him . . . '

'I hope he gets completely wet and miserable,' said Stephen Crane. 'I'm not going out to look at him — although it would be enjoyable to watch him gasping in that well.'

'Maybe he'll drown,' said Max Kerle.

'No. Possibly the well will accumulate about four feet of water but that's all. Enough to give him a really wet night. And it will be cold out there.' Stephen Crane chuckled unpleasantly.

'That and the hiding we gave him will make Jim Gallery rather ill. But he'll die tomorrow!'

'Who is gonna shoot him?' asked Kid Dawson. 'I'd like to fill him with lead. Look what he did to my brother . . . '

'Filled him with lead!' retorted Max Kerle and laughed viciously. It was his idea of a joke.

'You quit making out that that's funny!' growled Kid Dawson. 'You kinda like to get at me . . . '

'Waal, you rise to the bait every time.'

'Haven't you two any better brand of conversation?' snarled Stephen Crane. 'God, it's like having to listen to morons all the time!'

A silence fell over the three men.

The rain pelted down outside, making rivulets of water that sought outlet on lower levels of the rocky terrain. The sound of the sluicing deluge was continuous.

'Sure hope them horses are all right,' murmured Kid Dawson.

'They've got plenty of cover in that nook . . . '

'Sure would like to see that bastard gaspin' and flounderin' in that well,' went on Kid Dawson.

'Why don't you go take a look,' sneered Max Kerle. 'You'd get a wash into the bargain! Sure would do you a power of good — get rid of them desert fleas you got!'

'Why — you — ' Kid Dawson jerked into a threatening attitude, partly flinging his blanket to one side.

Stephen Crane said in sneering, bored tones, 'You two sound like childish idiots! God, what I've come down to! Now in my regiment . . . '

'The hell with your regiment!' Max Kerle flung the retort like a challenge. His eyes clashed with those of the other man.

'We are undoubtedly the most congenial company for each other,' persisted Stephen Crane. 'We regale each other with the most charming conversation!' His voice changed and cracked like a whip. 'I think after tonight we had better split up. We've accomplished our purpose. Gallery will be dead. I think we'd better ride separate ways. Too bad, Kerle, you failed to locate the missing Drago money . . . '

'Gallery sticks to his tale — Al Aston was robbed . . . '

The other man nodded. 'Could be true. You watched Gallery for months after the robbery. You say he never spent a cent above his average wages. To a man like Gallery, fond of the ladies and a night or two at the gaming tables, to have money close to hand and be unable to spend it would be almost intolerable.'

'I watched him in Laramie and Boulder,' said Kerle. 'He didn't know I was around. I tell you he ain't spent any real dinero for a long time . . . '

Stephen Crane nodded. 'Regrettable that this mystery will haunt you for the rest of your days — because Gallery is going to die — tomorrow!'

They had eaten and it was natural to feel drowsy because they had had a hard day in the saddle. They were well wrapped up and warm air circled back into the cave from the fire. Their personal animosities could not be maintained and so they fell asleep. The rain slashed down and scoured another layer of yellow dust from the bedrocks all around. The water gurgled energetically along a thousand crevices — down across the slabs of rock — along to the ancient well.

Jim Gallery stood chest high in the muddy swirl and stared at the round patch of sky which seemed just beyond his reach. He had yelled for help, but apparently no one heard him — or cared! The thunder had ceased. The wicked flashes of lightning had stopped cutting the dark night into weird sections.

But the rain fell in great sheets, and water poured into the well from a dozen different directions.

As he stared upwards, his dark hair became lank and clinging. His face, with its unmistakable Irish heritage, was lined grimly. He was scared. The well was filling. At this rate it would be over his head in a few more minutes. How long would it rain? He was as cold as a two-day corpse, but not quite as stiff. He felt gut-hungry. He knew he was physically weak and could only survive on a reserve of willpower.

Far from slackening off, the rain fell steadily, as if the floods had returned. The water in the well lapped to his chin and then into his mouth. He knew then it was time for him to re-learn an art he had seldom practised since boyhood. He'd have to learn to swim again!

He flicked off his boots then splashed out, remembering how to tread water. For thirty minutes he churned around like some drowning cur in a hole in the ground. Water poured in from above in about four main spouts. He tried to avoid these deluges. He found a side of the well that was relatively free of waterfalls. He stayed there and made a discovery. The rising water had carried him up to a point where the side of the well was a bit rough and this afforded him a precarious handgrip. He hung on, his feet churning like mad. He looked up to the edge of the well. It was still a long way off, beyond his most frantic reach. Would he drown when exhaustion overcame him?

Somewhere, miles away, the thunder rolled again. He heard the wind rise steadily again. A freak wind blew harshly for some time and brought the storm centre back over the hills. The rain came down with fresh vigour.

The men in the cave did not hear anything — or if they did they were so tired that background noises meant nothing to them. They slept on, soundly. The wind and rain lashed into their age-old barriers of rock cliff and bedrock. Finally, before the sun even showed the first feeble rays, the storm faded with surprising speed and the clouds dissipated.

The men in the cave stirred, instinctively knowing that this was another day, even through the dregs of sleep. One by one they got up and moved around in silence. Kid Dawson was the first to say, 'I'll go take a look at the doggone prisoner . . . '

'I'll come with you,' murmured Stephen Crane. 'By heaven, the earth smells sweet and cool!'

'Won't stay that way,' grunted Max Kerle. 'It'll heat up like an oven in those canyons and valleys. Let's go look at that tricky *hombre* . . . '

They walked out of the cave, across the beds of rock. Kerle and Dawson had shoulders hunched, hands rammed into pants pockets. Stephen Crane, as always, walked erectly, his arms swinging. None of the men had a gunbelt on or a rifle in hand.

'Sure hope that man ain't too cold

and wet to talk back!' sniggered Kid Dawson. 'Say, how're we goin' to kill him? Maybe we should draw lots, huh?'

'A knife in the guts is a real slow way,' grunted Max Kerle. 'Hell, I still ain't sure about him and that dinero . . . '

They tramped to the well and looked down. Surprise hit three grim faces. Yellow water lay placid and impenetrable to within three feet of the well rim. Nothing stirred in the murky depths.

'Waal, damn — he drowned!' yelled Kid Dawson, his blubbery face like a punch-ball.

'Yeah — he's at the bottom of that hole!' rasped Max Kerle. He began to laugh. 'Waal, so much for the rock-hard galoot, Jim Gallery! Drowned like some mangey polecat in a ditch!'

Stephen Crane stared, his eyes glinting. 'A dirty death — but don't be too sure, my friends. Still, I didn't think so much water would collect in that hole. And yet — I should have known

— it has been fashioned to take water from all points. Look at the weathered channels leading to it!'

Max Kerle whipped around. He glared at the hills, the rocky ledges and the stunted scrub bushes. 'Now, look, Crane — is he dead or not? What the blazes do you mean about not being too sure? How could a man get out of there? All that water . . .'

'The human body has buoyancy, you fool! Can't you swim? I guess you can't! Now a man who could keep afloat — '

Stephen Crane whipped around and began striding back, intent on an idea that had hit him like a landslide.

The other two men followed him, knowing he had some notion. They could see it in the grim way he strode on. And as they approached the nook where the horses had been tethered for the night, Max Kerle was the first to catch on. 'By thunder — the damned animals — '

'That's right,' snapped Stephen Crane, a sneer on his lips. 'You've cottoned on . . . '

'Horses!' yelped Kid Dawson, and he began to run. 'Hell . . . you don't mean . . . '

There was little need for a rush of useless words because when they rounded the rocky cleft everything was all too obvious.

The animals had gone!

'By God — he got outa that hole!' screamed Max Kerle. 'He rode out — with four damned horses!'

Stephen Crane whipped around to Kid Dawson as if the young man was some new rookie in the infantry ranks. The contempt in his tone was enough to poison any man against him. 'If I remember correctly, Dawson, you left your mount saddled. You couldn't be bothered to strip it. He'll have your animal, for sure. The others will be driven miles away by now. The one thing I can't be sure about is just how long he has been gone . . . '

'Long enough,' grunted Max Kerle. He glared up to the sun which was already ascending into the sky. 'It's gonna be as hot as all hell in this area — and us on foot.'

'We got guns!' argued Kid Dawson. 'We — '

'We've got to find that tricky swine before we can sight him with a gun!' sneered the other. 'You gone loco, Kid? Ain't you got no brains at all?'

'It weren't my idea to stick that swine in that hole!' shrilled Kid Dawson. 'I wanted him dead . . . '

'Are you implying that I've made a mess of things?' gritted Stephen Crane. 'There was no way of realizing so much water would funnel into the well — but I can see it now. Some Indians of long ago fashioned that hole for that express purpose — to catch a great deal of water in a short space of time.'

'So he kept afloat,' mused Max Kerle. 'And then climbed out when the water carried him up to the rim of the well. Gee, that goddamn hardcase! You know something? — the devil looks after Jim Gallery!' There was grudging admiration in his voice. 'But I'm goin' to kill that robbin' skunk some day all the same . . . '

'Is that so?' Kid Dawson had resented the other man's comments on his intelligence. 'You goin' to figure out how we can walk forty miles to Delta?'

Stephen Crane whipped around, assuming his old stature of authority over these two men.

'We've got to get started. We might be able to find the horses. Gallery might drive them off after a few miles . . . '

'He won't!' sneered Max Kerle. 'He won't run them loose under ten miles. I know that clever coyote. And they'll stray. We could be two days trackin' down them mounts.'

'I know that,' said Stephen Crane coldly. 'But there is a chance that one of the animals ran off — out of Gallery's control — and is not too far away at this very moment. At any rate, we've got to start moving. Unless you plan to take up residence here . . . '

'Real fancy talk!' sneered Max Kerle. 'And that damned accent! When the hell are you goin' to talk like a real westerner?'

'My style of speech shouldn't concern you!'

With that rapped comment, which was subtly designed to push Max Kerle right back into his place, Stephen Crane walked back to the cave where they had left their gear. Here were piled saddles — with the exception of the one owned by Kid Dawson — but they were useless. Still, they had water canteens and plenty of water outside. They had guns and rifles and some food. But all they had for transportation were their legs — and in the hot, arid conditions of the badlands between this spot and Delta a man could become mighty weary, possibly lamed, and if he had no water, he could be quickly dehydrated.

Three grim men made preparations to move on. But not before there was some debate about the wisdom of tramping on oven-hot land during the time the sun was at its highest.

'We could move at night — be a damn sight cooler,' said Max Kerle.

'We'd never see those horses if we delay another eight hours,' rapped Stephen Crane.

'Ain't no guarantee we'll ever sight 'em . . . '

'I know. But at night we won't even see Gallery's tracks.'

'He'll head for Delta — where else?'

'There is Salida — not that far to the east . . . '

'Too damn far for three *hombres* on foot!' sneered Max Kerle. 'You know every blasted mile counts . . . '

'Delta, then,' commented the ex-army man.

'He's got no guns — and no grub,' Kid Dawson pointed out. 'He ain't got all the aces. What'll he do for water, huh?'

'You left your rig on that hoss,' grated Max Kerle. 'And you had two water bottles slung on it. Need to say any more?'

'He can ride that animal to death and make it quickly to Delta — or he can take it easy for two days,' added Stephen Crane.

'He'd have taken a horse and ridden bareback in any case,' raged Kid Dawson. 'Lack of a saddle wouldn't've stopped Gallery . . . '

'Lack of water canteens might!' Max Kerle's retort came back like a Colt slug spitting through thin air. 'What the hell! Let's light out! Of all the dadblasted luck! We should've drilled that devil last night . . . '

3

Girl in the Night

Jim Gallery rode grimly and tiredly, sitting the saddle like a hunched up old man. He was tired as all hell. He had struggled for his life all night, fighting to survive, swimming like a rat in a barrel. He had hauled himself out of the well, blessing the torrential rain that had threatened to drown him. He had made it.

He had silently crept to the horses; his stockinged feet making him as silent as an Indian. Fearful lest the animals might snicker, he had held his breath while he led them away.

At a wise distance he had got aboard the nag which was still saddled. He noted the water canteens and stopped at the nearest creek to fill them. Then, with the rope coiled on the saddlehorn, he had made a lead rope for the other horses. In this manner he had ridden on, guided by the position of the rising sun, for about three hours.

Then, because the three other horses were slowing him, he had released them and sent them running with a wild shout. If Stephen Crane and his partners found the horses after that interval and distance, they would be very lucky — and too late! But as the sun rose and the heat became fierce, he had to resort more and more to the canteens. The animal needed water — very important. So he stopped occasionally.

He was hungry, with the gnawing feeling that comes with a really empty gut. There was nothing in this wilderness to chew on. He could not even kill a lizard and chew the raw flesh. He was weary, his bruises beginning to ache like some torment. He'd taken a beating. Grim, and cursing the land, he allowed the horse to plod on, at its own pace because this was the wisest course.

His stockinged feet pressed against hot stirrups and he wished he had his boots — but they were water-logged, at the bottom of the Indian well.

He had gotten away from death by the skin of his teeth, leaving behind three men who would vow renewed vengeance. They'd more than hate his guts now!

He rode all day and used a canteen of water. He led the horse into some broken land that showed signs of greenery. He spotted some clumps of juniper, hanging with berries, and knew there was water close by. The land slanted into a deep little vee, and there was the spring, bubbling between rocks, a mystery in this silent land. With the rains of the previous night feeding the underground channels, the spring was running full and there was grass, tender and fresh, for the horse. Pity he, too, couldn't eat grass — because there was nothing else and he possessed neither gun nor knife with which to kill anything that moved.

He sat that evening, with the sun ready to sink fast, his feet in a pool, his face bathed. The cuts and bruises had reached their fully swollen state and his ribs still ached where he had been kicked. But he was alive and he'd get over all this. Still, he did look like some battered pugilist.

He was hitching the horse for the night, contemplating a quick getaway long before sun-up, when he heard the slow clop-clop of hoofs. He whipped around, crouched, his brain leaping through the possibilities. Crane and his cronies could not have caught up with him. There was only one horse . . . so it was some lone rider . . .

He wasn't really prepared to see a girl mounted on a big black mare — but she came swiftly into view. Their eyes locked, questioningly, warily. She noted his lack of hardware, his puffed features, his lack of boots. She was a girl of fast reactions. As for Jim Gallery, there was some relief. He even managed a smile — which hurt.

'Howdy, ma'am!' It was merely an acknowledgement.

'Who are you? What are you doing here?' There was some fear in her questions. She sat the sleek black horse with some control and authority, but she was sitting side-saddle. She wore a long black skirt and a white blouse. Her dark hair, gleaming like a raven's wing, was coiled carefully at the back of her head. She was tanned, but her skin was as clear as dew on a spring morning.

'I'm Jim — ' He paused. 'That's enough . . . I'm here because I need to rest — and this is the best spot I've encountered in the past twenty miles.'

'You've come across the badlands?'

'If you really got to know — yes. And you, miss? Why're you out ridin' at this time of night? It'll be really dark with hardly any moon in about twenty minutes . . . '

'I have to ride,' she burst out. Her coolness seemed to leave her for the first time. 'I have to get to Delta . . . '

'That's a long way.'

'I know. But I need to get there as fast as I can. I have to find a doctor.' She flung him a fast, shrewd glance. 'You're not one of the gang. You're not one of the men who shot my father . . . '

He nodded, tried to smile again. 'That's right, so far. I'm not one of any gang. I'm a bit of a loner. What's wrong with your pa — apart from the obvious?'

'He's losing blood quickly!' Her composure faltered. 'The bullet hit a vein, in his shoulder, and I tried to stem the flow — but — but — '

'Are you livin' around here some-wheres?' he said incredulously. 'So near to the wastelands? Why?'

'What's that to you?' she snapped. Then in some confusion, she stam-mered: 'I'm sorry — I didn't mean to be rude — but — '

Jim Gallery moved purposefully. 'We're wastin' time, miss. How far away do you live?'

'Just two miles or so from here . . . '

'Let's get goin'. If he's bleeding badly time is important.'

'But he needs a real doctor . . . '

'I've done plenty of doctorin' — where bullet wounds are concerned — ain't so good with measles or childbirth — but slugs I done taken plenty out!' He vaulted stiffly to the saddle of his horse. 'And maybe you got some food at home?'

'We've got plenty — yes . . . '

'I'm so hungry I could chew on a dead pack-horse and enjoy it. And maybe you got a pair of boots — maybe your pa's spare pair — iffen he's got feet as big as mine!'

'He's a big man.' She looked carefully at him again. 'You've been in some trouble. You've been fighting; your face is bruised — '

He wheeled his horse. The animal snorted, resentful, reluctant to leave the green grass. He nudged it hard in the ribs with his knees and, with the girl, they sped into the rapidly darkening night.

A thought occurred to him. 'This gang who shot your pa . . . how many galoots? And why? Why'd they shoot him?'

Her voice carried back through the cooler night air. 'I'll tell you later . . . '

'When you've figured me out!' he rapped and grinned. 'All right, it's a deal. Boots and grub — and I'll do my best for your pa. Then I'll ride on. Seems we're both lucky. You got a name, miss — '

'I'm Helen Mackay. My father is known to his few friends as Bert . . . we live alone . . . '

Jim Gallery managed to get his tired horse into a full lope. 'You know, that was a mighty dangerous trip you were contemplating,' he said. 'You — alone — at night twenty miles to Delta! Your pa could bleed to death long afore you got back. And what about this damned gang? Will they make a return visit?'

'I said I'd tell you more later.' She paused, half-turned her cool, pretty face. 'I am grateful, Mr . . . '

'You might as well know I'm Jim Gallery . . . '

'You're a cowhand?'

'Nope. A drifter — a hardcase . . . '

'Oh!' She became silent, and the horses moved as swiftly as they dared on the darkened trail. After half a mile, the girl swung her animal towards some rising hills which were covered in clumps of wild sage and prickly chaparral. After another half mile, they rode a narrow goat like track through rocky outcrops that stood up like sentinels, twice the height of a barn. Jim Gallery wondered just why this girl and her father were living out here in this wild land.

'When did your pa get shot?' he asked her.

'Only an hour ago. At first I tried to stop the bleeding. But I just couldn't do it. I — I — got a bit scared and decided to ride for a doc . . . '

As they rode he noted the jagged rocks that stood up like giant teeth in all directions. Wind and rain had scoured this area for hundreds of years, leaving the hard rocks, cutting gullies in all directions.

And then quite suddenly he spotted the shack in the gathering gloom. The structure was pretty ramshackle, made of logs, lengths of clapboard, with a sod roof, and a porch of sun bleached, unpainted wood. He saw the stone chimney stack at one side, useful for cold winter nights, and a rough corral to the right of the place. As he rode up and dismounted and hitched the leathers around a tierail he saw the huge heaps of chipped stone. There were five such piles, all to the right of the shack, near the rocky cliff that faced the house. He formed a few ideas, but there wasn't time for a look around. He had to attend a wounded man. He had a feeling Helen Mackay would never have brought him or anyone like him to this place had it not been for her father.

And then, seconds later, he was inside the place and bending over the oldster. He saw a big man, all of six feet, broad-shouldered, with plenty of weight. He had white, bushy hair and a thick beard of the same hue. His wound was really bothering him. He grimaced with pain — wracked eyes when he saw Jim Gallery. His shoulder was wrapped in strips of white cloth which were now red with blood.

'Who the heck is this, Helen?'

'He's going to help you, Father.'

The old man grunted, snarled with pain, and writhed. 'All . . . right . . . can you get this blamed slug . . . out . . . mister . . . ?'

Jim Gallery began working without a word. He unwrapped the red bandages; looked at the nasty wound for a moment. The slug had torn into a major vein. Bert Mackay had lost plenty of blood.

The next ten minutes were punctuated by snarling moans from the old man, a few rapped commands from Jim Gallery. Helen brought him a sharp, pointed knife. The steel was finely honed and good for the job. She also brought him iodine, some pads of cloth and fresh strips for bandages. There was no whisky in the shack; nothing the old man could take to dull the pain of the improvised operation. He just had to get relief in issuing his harsh moans and yells as the steel dug deep. Helen held him down. Jim Gallery worked as quickly as he could. The slug was eventually extracted and then the restraining pads and bandages applied. By the time this was done, Bert Mackay was limp, and he lay back with closed eyes, only a slight moan bubbling from his lips.

'He'll be all right,' said Jim Gallery, his hands wet with blood. 'If the bleeding stops — and I figure it will — he'll be up and around inside three days — but he won't be able to use that arm for some time.' He sluiced his hands in a bucket of cold water. Helen Mackay handed him a coarse towel. 'Now what about the grub? Not to mention the boots?'

'You're welcome,' she said quietly.

'That's all I need — unless you got a gun you don't want. And a bed for the night. I'll be on my way at sunup . . . '

There were other chores to do, such as a feed for his horse. He removed the saddle, giving the mount some freedom. He stared again at the heaps of stone chips but the night had become really gloomy. So, shrugging, he went indoors again. Helen had made him a bed on the living room floor. There were only two other rooms, and she used one as her bedroom.

A few minutes later she had cooked him some grub. He attacked the heap of bacon and beans, fried bread and apple tart like a starving man. He shovelled the grub into him, and then paused over the mug of hot coffee. 'Sorry. I was more than hungry . . . empty . . . and damned tired. I'll turn in, if you don't mind.'

Her eyes gleamed in the yellow lamplight. 'You don't want to ask questions?'

'No more than you want to ask me.'

'I'm grateful.'

'Sure. So am I, Miss Helen.'

Twenty minutes later he was sound asleep, like a man who has sunk into temporary oblivion. In the other room, Helen Mackay lay with eyes wide open, wondering about this stranger.

Who was Jim Gallery? Dirty, unshaven, his face showing many marks of a recent beating, foodless and gunless — without boots — in these badlands — was he a dangerous drifter or just another man?

She thought her father would be all right now . . . a good thing she had met Jim Gallery . . . but the robbery rankled . . . her father would be impossible to live with for the next week or so. He'd be in a real rage. And with good reason — months of work for nothing! Just to enrich two no-good hellions who had appeared from nowhere and demanded the gold. And when her father had rightly resisted, they had shot him — not to kill, because they had wanted to make him talk. And when her father had staggered back with blood pouring from his shoulder, she had told the mean-looking rannigans where to find the cache of gold. She had feared they would kill her father . . .

★　★　★

Jim Gallery stirred when the sun had been playing on him for some time through the window. He lay, looking around. His clothes lay in a heap — the worse for wear brown pants, the black shirt and leather vest. They'd been soaked and then dried in the sun. Blood had congealed on them; sweat had permeated them during the day-time ride.

Somehow the thought of the cool, clear-faced Helen Mackay lying in the other room could not be dispelled from his mind. He realized she was a pretty young woman, attractive to any man who had time to think about her. In a way, she reminded him of Molly Peterson; the same lithe figure and dark hair. Maybe Molly had married some other *hombre* by now.

He got up. He dressed, put on the boots Helen had found for him. They fitted reasonably well; better than nothing. He ran a hand over his stubble; maybe her father had a razor. It might be a good idea if he smartened up a bit. In town he could look a real dandy, given the right clothes. Well, when he hit Delta there'd be some changes. He had some money in the bank there. He'd buy some gear, a new horse, guns, and then he'd go look for Henry Carslake. The tricky swine was somewhere — with the dinero from the Drago Cattlemen's Bank!

4

Death — and Gold

The three men were mean and bitter by the end of the first day's march over the bad terrain. True, they had plenty of water and some grub in the saddle-bags they had slung over their shoulders, but that was only a slight help as they stumbled along in their high-heeled riding boots. They were *en route* to Delta, sure enough, and had seen the tracks of the four horses right up to the spot where Jim Gallery had evidently dispersed them. They then wasted much time trying to spot the animals from some high ground, but to no avail.

'We'll camp,' stated Stephen Crane, his grey moustache and face powdered with fine dust. 'Right here. With our backs to those damned rocks. That was always a good principle in India . . . '

'This is Colorado, *amigo!*' sneered Max Kerle. 'And the Cheyenne are peaceful from right here to Bent's Fort — but if you go south you're in Apache country and that's different.'

'I do not need your educational efforts, Kerle!' the retort came angrily. 'I merely said we'd camp here . . . '

'That damned snake, Jim Gallery, is miles ahead of us!' moaned Kid Dawson. 'And tomorrow — with his mount fresh — he'll push right into Delta. If he's got money stashed away in that burg, he could take the stage to Denver — or anywhere — but I'll find him. I got my brother to think about.'

'Gallery killed him fair and square,' sneered Max Kerle. 'Take a tip from that, Kid!'

'Hell, I'm sick and tired of you tryin' to rile me!' Kid Dawson suddenly screamed, and his hand flashed down to his hip. He had only one gun — and even so he did not lift it. He just oozed hatred of the other man.

'Simmer down, my man!' Stephen

Crane rapped out, disgust lying thick in his annoying accent.

'I ain't your man, damn you!' Kid Dawson whipped around again, glared at the tall, older man. 'I'm sick to hell of you, too!'

'If you ever catch up with Jim Gallery,' said Max Kerle, 'don't lose your cool — because he'll bury you! I know him.'

'I'm beginning to wonder why we ever decided to hunt Gallery together,' said Stephen Crane calmly. 'I doubt if we have much in common.'

'You figured there was some chance of learnin' about the Drago dinero!' Max Kerle couldn't resist that dig. 'It wasn't all on account of how Gallery offended you by marching you in for bounty.'

'How very perceptive.' Stephen Crane sat down, his back to a rock, and began to look through his saddle-bags for some food. 'But you know Gallery would die before talking. Oh, the devil take this conversation. I wish to God I was with my regiment! At least my brother officers behaved like gentlemen . . . '

'Yeah . . . right up to the time they drummed you out!' Max Kerle laughed grittily. He sat down, placed his rifle close by. 'I need shut-eye. The hell with you two . . . '

He did not see the disdain in Stephen Crane's eyes; he was lying back, relaxed. He thought he would find a new partner some day — if they ever finished the job of filling Gallery with lead. Right now he was stuck with Crane and Dawson. Damn them both!

Kid Dawson walked around the cluster of rocks; peered into the night. His hate for Jim Gallery was very real, more acute because he had known they should have killed the man the moment they found him. He blamed Crane for Jim Gallery's escape. His fool idea about the well had been responsible for that.

Kid Dawson stared into the night, his fist clenched, his fleshy face an ugly mask. He was about to return to the cluster of rocks and settle down for the night when he thought he saw something move out there in the darkness. He froze. Then he knew it couldn't be Gallery. He was having delusions about the hardcase. But there was something — and a moment later he heard the sound of slowly moving horses. Horses! The very thing they needed!

He listened for some moments. Trail-wise, he knew there were two riders. What in tarnation were they poking around for after sundown?

Kid Dawson hurried back to the others. 'Listen . . . horses! Out there!'

After a few moments of listening, there was no doubt. The two riders were in actual fact coming closer.

'Let's get them!' snarled Max Kerle. 'We need horses . . . '

'Could be lawmen,' commented Stephen Crane. 'Night riding! Now I wonder . . . '

Max Kerle was wasting no time. He lay flat behind a convenient boulder, facing the direction of the hoof falls, and he had his rifle sighted in that direction.

Taking a tip the other two adopted the same position. They lay like snakes ready to strike.

The slow clop-clop of shod hoofs came closer and then the dark outline of the horses and riders were suddenly visible shapes in the night. Three vicious rifles levelled, sighted, and then without mercy, caring nothing about the identity of their victims, the guns spoke.

The night was shattered by the sharp crack of the rifles. The guns sang out their deadly, brutal message and the two riders toppled from saddles with almost comical finality. As the reverberations of the guns flashed across the silent land, the horses spooked and raced in different directions. For a moment or two one of the riders was trapped in a stirrup and dragged some distance. This caused the horse to veer, and it came right towards the three bushwhackers. That was nice and handy. Kid Dawson made a grab for trailing leathers; Max Kerle flung his arms around the horse's neck and dragged it to a halt.

The second animal took some hunting, but three men, determined to succeed, circled the frightened horse. Eventually it was caught, by Kid Dawson, who figured he was having a triumphant time. The two animals were pacified, brought back to the cluster of rocks and hobbled and the saddles and other gear examined. The result was satisfactory — another two rifles in saddle holsters, jerky meat and blanket rolls. Then Stephen Crane and Max Kerle went out to look at the two dead men. It was mostly curiosity; it was always possible they might know the rannigans.

They made two discoveries. One man was still alive, but only just. They didn't care about that fragile fact; but the second find was interesting. The nearly dead man, lean and grim-faced, had two sacks of gold nuggets tied securely around his waist. They were very heavy and most men would have fixed them to the saddlehorns, but it seemed this individual liked the feel of gold close to him. The find amazed and excited Max Kerle and Crane, and they took another look at the other dead man, who was lying some distance away. Previously they had merely toed him over with a foot. And sure enough they found that he too, was laden with two sacks of gold.

The two men knew all about the sight and feel of gold. Max Kerle had done a spot of ore-digging and panning in his varied career.

Stephen Crane turned the dying man over; then sat him up. But it wasn't an act of mercy. He was curious. 'Where did you find this gold? Are you prospectors?'

The man stared with wild, pain-wracked eyes. 'Prospectors — hell . . . me and Buddy . . . just picked it up . . . get me to a doc . . . don't leave me . . . you can have my gold . . . just get me to a doc . . . '

'All right, tell me more,' said Stephen Crane soothingly. 'I'll patch you up. I'm rather good at the medical stuff, you know.'

'Don't let me die . . .

'I won't old man. Now tell me, where did you get the gold if you didn't mine it?'

'Took it . . . from the old galoot . . . and his daughter . . . at the Yellow Stones . . . '

'Yellow Stones? Where is that?'

'Broken country . . . just a few miles west of here . . . me and Buddy was headin' out for town . . . '

'An old man and his daughter? Out here?'

'They've got a mine . . . guess there's more gold . . . we just lit out with the four small sacks . . . oh . . . God . . . I think I'm goin' to die . . . don't let me die . . . '

'You are dead!' snarled Stephen Crane. He rammed the man back as if he would crush him into the earth.

With that, he and Max Kerle untied the small sacks of gold and carried them away, along with the two from the other man. Max Kerle was excited; he was thinking — gold, horses! Sheer luck! The kind of luck the range wanderer dreamed about. Four sacks of gold, two horses — and three men! Did it have to be shared?

Max Kerle did not realize that Stephen Crane was thinking along the same lines. Cruelly, he decided there was one man too many in the outfit, but he wasn't sure which one would have to go. And quite possibly the question would have to be decided later! Yes, what was it the dying rannigan had said about the possibility of more gold?

There was no hiding the finds from Kid Dawson when they got back to the cluster of rocks, the hobbled horses and other gear that comprised their base. For one thing, Crane and Kerle were so excited they just had to examine the bags of gold again, feel the weight and assess the value.

'More where this came from!' said Stephen Crane. 'That man said there was a possibility of more gold — in some place called the Yellow Stones. Do you know of it?'

'Yellow Stones!' exclaimed Kid Dawson. 'Why, that ain't far from here. Reckon about ten miles . . . ain't much now we got horses . . . '

'Two horses,' murmured Stephen Crane. 'For three men. Still, no doubt we could reach the place.'

Kid Dawson looked at the sacks of gold and greed flickered across his blubbery face. 'Yeah, but what about Gallery?'

'We'll deal with him — some day.'

'He could get clear to hell!'

'We'll find him. With gold behind us we can track down any man,' retorted the other.

'I sure want to kill Gallery . . . '

'I like gold,' murmured Stephen Crane, and he lifted a sack again with a speculative gleam in his eyes.

'This is sure our lucky night!' rasped Max Kerle. 'Four sacks of gold and — ' He nearly said three men, but that had implications that were better left unsaid.

'We'll set off for this Yellow Stones area in the morning,' stated Stephen Crane as if his decision was final.

★ ★ ★

Jim Gallery did not know why he lingered in the place. He had had breakfast, which Helen Mackay had cooked for him, and he'd shaved, a painful business considering the state of his face. Still, he felt and looked much better, except for the fact that his shirt and pants were a mess. He wet his hair from a jug of cold water Helen brought him from the spring outside and tried to smooth down the thick, dark locks. He stared into a cracked little mirror; saw the dark Irish face and grinned faintly. Maybe in a day or two he'd be his old self, ready for some good food, a drink and a hand of cards — but that would be best done a long way from Delta!

She came into the living room and smiled at him. 'My father seems a lot letter already . . . '

'I guess he's a tough old *hombre*.'

'He's a hard man,' she admitted. 'He has to be — ' She broke off.

Jim Gallery grinned. 'Mining is hard graft, sure thing. Do you like living out here? I mean, this is no place for a gal.'

'I have to — with my father.'

'I didn't know there was gold to be found around here.'

'So you've guessed!' She sighed. 'I might as well tell you — two men rode up and shot my father — not to kill — they wanted to make him talk . . . and then I had to tell them where we had cached some gold. Four small sacks . . . nuggets . . . I don't know how they got to know about us . . . '

'Stories get around — where gold is concerned,' said Jim Gallery. 'Men get greedy . . . '

She regarded him steadily. 'There isn't any more — except in the ground — and it is very hard work just to win it.'

'You don't have to worry about me,' he said quietly. 'I'm goin' . . . '

'I've told you the truth about this place.' She paused. 'And you? A man without food or guns or boots? A man with bruises?'

'I've told you — I'm Jim Gallery. Just a man ridin' by.'

'You're running from other men!'

She had only her intuition as a guide, and her comment was so near the truth that Jim Gallery grinned in admission, and she saw the expression. She turned away, and the next moment there was a growling shout from the bedroom in which her father lay. She hurried to see him.

Jim Gallery went out to look at the horse. He saddled the animal again, without any haste. He stared around the scene. It was in many ways a hideout and right off the beaten track.

It was occurring to him that Stephen Crane and his companions, if they were still pressing on to Delta, would take a trail many miles from this place and never give it a thought.

In a way, he could lie low here for a few days. Maybe it was an idea. Looking for Harry Carslake was a long term job in any case. The robbing, murdering skunk was somewhere in the wild land between the Colorado River and the San Juan River — that he knew from information received — but exactly where he was holed-up he wasn't sure about. Certainly not in any town. He had asked a thousand questions of travellers, men he knew, who had taken stage journeys, men range-wandering and men dodging the law.

No one had seen Harry Carslake in any town. But he had been seen in the wild, sparsely populated land between the rivers, that triangular-shaped chunk of territory, where the peaceful Cheyenne and the warlike Apache met. And if he was there, he was hiding, and he would have the twenty thousand dollars which had been formerly part of the big assets of the Drago Cattlemen's Bank.

That dinero did not belong to Harry Carslake. They had merely lifted it. Al Aston was dead. Harry had killed him. That hadn't been part of the deal. Harry had been told just to get the money and meet Jim Gallery later, but Harry had figured on death and a double-cross.

It was all a setup that would have to be trimmed with some justice some day. Harry Carslake could not be allowed to get away with it. At the same time, Max Kerle must not be allowed to suspect anything. He didn't even know Harry Carslake.

As Jim Gallery rubbed the horse down and tightened the cinch, the girl walked up to him. 'You are leaving?'

'I should move on . . . '

'You can stay for another meal. I owe you a lot — my father seems a bit improved — although his temper is bad — and the bleeding has stopped.'

'He'll be all right, Miss Helen . . . '

'Will you stay?' She seemed eager. Then, realizing she was pressing him, she blushed and lowered her eyes. He knew it was the first time he had seen her lose her composure, and he smiled.

'I'll stick around,' he said. 'And I'll tell you the story of my life — all the goldarned wicked parts.'

'I don't think you are wicked . . . '

'Miss — you sure don't know me!' And it was no joke. He had done too many lawless things; he wouldn't tell her the half of it.

There was the bank robbery, with Max Kerle and Al Aston. She wouldn't like to hear about that. He had killed Kid Dawson's brother — fair and square — but the ranny was dead! Hardly a nice topic of conversation to hand to a young girl. He had gone for Stephen Crane because there was a price on the man's head. Sure, he was a hardcase. Maybe it had all started way back, when his father had been killed during a card game, and when his mother had got in the way of a stagecoach and four horses driven by a drunken ribbon-handler. As a kid he had been kicked around. He had stolen his first gun.

'A penny for them!' She smiled into his eyes.

She was too close, too sweet and clear-skinned for a man who had experienced only Molly Peterson apart from the saloon girls. He impulsively put out a hand and touched the bare skin of her arm. It was like an electric shock just to realize how soft and lovely she was. His hand stayed on her arm. Looking into her brown eyes, he saw them flicker. Then he put out his other arm — and gathered her into his embrace. In a second she was pressed close to him and his mouth was on her lips, kissing her almost savagely.

It was only her struggles that brought him to his senses. He let her go — after the shattering discovery that she was beautiful and warm and desirable. He stood, lines biting deeply into his face. 'I'm sorry! I shouldn't have done that!'

'I — I — shouldn't have let you.'

'You didn't! I just grabbed you!'

'I could have slapped your face — but I didn't want to hurt you.'

He half-turned. 'I guess I'll have to go now. Just don't think too badly about me. I — I — I'm not used to girls as pretty and as nice as you! I'm just a man . . . been hitting saddle . . . and hard riding for so long I don't know what decent livin' is about. I'll go!'

'Will you come back?' It was an impulsive question which was too daring by far! She bit her lip.

He smiled. 'That I might, Helen. I haven't many real friends . . . maybe I should cultivate a few . . . And you — don't you ever get into town? There's two good drapery emporiums in Delta — kinda interest a gal lookin' for finery — and two good hotels, with restaurants . . . '

'Oh, I've been in with my father! It is nice to see people and — and — other women! We go to church when we're there! Originally, we came from the Green River country in Wyoming.'

'I know the place. Been around Laramie . . . ' He turned to the horse and patted the creature's head. 'Look after your pa . . . '

★ ★ ★

He was riding through the rocky gullies, away from the half-hidden shack, out towards the open land. Helen Mackay was right behind him on a saddled horse which she had taken from their corral at the last moment, deciding to see him off. She wasn't riding side-saddle this time, but astride, which was more suited to the life she was leading. She wore blue jeans and a checked shirt and seemed more girlish as a result. They rode behind the last of the giant rock sentinels, with the thorny cactus at the base, and paused for a moment. Jim Gallery was about to speak when he saw the dark speck of a rider on the distant slope of land.

He and Helen waited. The man and horse were making directly for the thrust of rocks. As the horse plodded on, the blotch of white on its head bobbing regularly, there was something familiar about the man's shape to Jim Gallery. And then he knew. This *hombre* approaching was the sheriff of Delta, Mack Slater, a tubby man with an honest way of dealing with his problems.

What the devil brought him out here? What was behind his direct track to the broken, rocky patch of land? Who was he looking for? A lawman wouldn't ride all this way merely to pass the time of day! Mack Slater had something on his mind. One thing was for sure, the man did not have anything on Jim, no knowledge of his lawless past. He'd been a good boy in Delta . . .

5

The Murderous Three

The three mean companions were, for the time being, in a good humour as they rode slowly over the undulating, arid land. They even bandied jokes with each other. Kid Dawson rode up behind Stephen Crane on one horse and Max Kerle enjoyed the comfort of one saddle to himself. The ten miles or so to the Yellow Stones district was going to be pleasant. There was, it seemed, some tonic effect in the very feel of a sack of gold! Two were slung from Stephen Crane's saddle pommel and two with Max Kerle. The men were trusting each other — temporarily!

The sun climbed steadily, causing heat shimmers to dance on the horizon. The ride was a slow one, stopping repeatedly so that the men could drink water. They were even generous to the two horses; that was actually an essential. They still had plenty of miles to traverse and memory of the footsore trek from the Indian well was still with them.

'Gold, huh!' Max Kerle bawled. 'Ain't that somethin', Kid?'

'Seems good . . . '

'Possibly more at this Yellow Stones place,' remarked Stephen Crane. 'It's worth looking into, I'd say.'

'Howsabout the old galoot and his daughter — like that dyin' feller said — there's an old man and a girl.'

'If they give any trouble,' said Stephen Crane coldly, 'we shall have to eliminate them.'

'I don't get why them two fellers didn't take all the gold when they was about it,' pursued Max Kerle. 'I mean, Crane, how do we know there's more?'

'That man said there was more. He was dying . . . '

'Sure — and maybe he was just talkin' wild. I just don't figure why they didn't take all the gold — that's all . . . '

'He said more where it came from,' ruminated Stephen Crane. 'I suppose that could mean anything. Well, do we look at this Yellow Stones place — or press on to Delta and what passes for civilization in this confounded country?'

'You puttin' this to the vote and not issuing orders as usual?' asked Max Kerle sarcastically.

'I'd like to plug Jim Gallery,' hissed Kid Dawson. A mask-like twist settled on his fleshy face. He was working up his hate again. 'He'll be ahead of us all the way if we stop off at this Yellow Stones place. Ain't we got enough gold?'

'A man can never accumulate enough gold,' sneered Stephen Crane. 'Damn, if I really struck it rich — I mean real wealth — I'd sail for England and buy myself a proper estate befitting my previous position in life! Do you men know what it is to have servants only too glad to obey one's slightest whim?

Could you appreciate the theatre in London or the exclusiveness of a good gentleman's club? I doubt it.'

'We ain't got your education — Colonel — sir,' Max Karle ripped back.

'My ma was educated — ' began Kid Dawson.

'But you ain't never knowed who the hell your pa was!' Max Kerle threw back and he roared with laughter.

The two horses were moving steadily, climbing a long, gradual rise of the land, going in the direction indicated by Kid Dawson who insisted he knew where to find the Yellow Stones location. As they breasted the rise the horses were halted while Max Kerle pointed a long, dirty-sleeved arm to the bed of the valley below.

'Hell and tarnation — look at that!'

The yellow sandy land, with its sprinkling of tufts of bunch-grass, bore a dark patch right in the centre. About fifty horses were placidly grouped together in a large circle and cropping at the browned grass. There were solids, big blacks and browns, and there were a number of multi-coloured mustangs. The solids were big horses, about fifteen hands high, and the others were smaller, wiry creatures. A man on a saddled horse sat hunched, apparently watching the remuda, content to sit out there in the sun. To one side in the shade of a large boulder, a smaller figure sat. After a second glance by the three men on the rise, they came to the conclusion the smaller figure was a boy. He was clad in a floppy, battered stetson and dusty range clothes. The man on the saddled horse wore a buckskin jacket and black trousers tucked into scuffed boots.

No more details were apparent to the three ruffians on the rise. There was too much distance. But probably the man on the horse, watching the herd, wore a gunbelt and sixgun. He didn't turn his horse, or even more, so they could not be sure.

'Now don't that take some beatin'!' exclaimed Max Kerle. 'What the devil are they doin' out here with a pack of horseflesh that size?'

'That's a neat question,' said Stephen Crane. 'Seeing that this is the fringe of the badlands. Who would want to drive a remuda in this direction? He's off the proper trail . . . '

'Maybe he's lost,' muttered Kid Dawson. 'Looks like a mustanger — with his son. Say, I hear there's plenty of horses in the San Juan Mountains!'

'There's plenty right here,' said Max Kerle wickedly. 'Can you figure what they're worth, partner? I can see two that look real beauts! Worth a hundred dollars in the right market! You know that, Kid?'

'I know horses,' said the other defensively.

'Fifty — prime mounts — and only a man and his son,' said Max Kerle reflectively. 'Say, this badland country is mighty interestin'! First it's gold — and now a herd of prime horseflesh!'

'Have we got time?' snapped Stephen

Crane. 'Hell, we want to look at this gold worked by some old man and a girl, and then we want to obliterate Gallery — '

'We can do the lot,' said Max Kerle.

Kid Dawson protested. 'What the blazes are you gettin' at! You figure to steal that damned remuda?'

'We could do with another mount,' argued the lanky ruffian. 'And I tell you that herd is worth dinero. All we have to do is drive them to Delta — and we don't want the mustanger and his kid around to argue otherwise when we hit town.'

'We could drive them to Yellow Stones and take a day off to look into this gold,' commented Stephen Crane. 'Then it's an easy ride to Delta. All is grist that comes to the mill!'

'Oh, goddamnit what about Gallery?' yelled the Kid. 'Ain't we after that bastard or not? He'll get plumb away to hell and gone.'

'We've got time,' said the army man. 'You have no patience, Dawson. Have you forgotten the weeks it has taken us to track Gallery in any case? Another week won't matter; we'll get him, rest assured. You'll have your revenge.'

'Let's ride down — nice and easy like. We don't want to scare 'em.' Max Kerle tugged on his leathers. 'We're just three honest Joes what's lost a horse and we're headin' for Delta and our humble families. That sound good, Crane?'

'Slightly nauseating — but, then, I know you, Kerle. Yes, let's ride down . . . easily . . . we'll get the man's story — before we deal with him and the boy.'

'Dead folks don't tell no tales,' muttered the hawklike man.

With Kid Dawson grumbling incoherently about the wasted time and the sufficiency of the gold, the two animals plodded down into the valley. Max Kerle even waved in friendly fashion to the mustanger. When they were closer, Stephen Crane, equally evil, shouted a greeting.

'Hello, my friend, you seem to be off-trail with your herd! Are you bound for Delta? We're three wanderers . . . we've lost a horse . . . could you sell us a horse . . . we'll pay a fair price . . . '

The man in the buckskin jacket straightened his back and stared with a long but not unfriendly look. Then he nudged his mount towards the three men on the two horses, and at the same time the slight figure rose from the shade of the boulder. The floppy old stetson was pushed back to reveal fair curly hair. At that moment Max Kerle saw that the dusty range clothes could not conceal entirely a feminine figure.

'By heck, it's a gal!' He quickly altered his gloating tone. 'Why, howdy, missy — sure did take you for a boy!'

'I'm Delia Breen — and this is my father — known to most as Walt.' The girl regarded the newcomers with a steady, curious expression.

The mustanger was a man of about forty-five, it seemed, to the three hardcases. He was dark-bearded, broad-shouldered, a body-hard man. He said, 'We ain't off-trail, mister. I ain't that stupid. Truth is we've driven these horses in a wide loop. I've been hunting mustangs in the San Juan hills and buying some other stock here and there. We had a deal to sell 'em in Silverton — but that fell through so I figured to skirt these badlands and get to Delta. I happen to know the cavalry is in Delta and lookin' for good mounts.'

'Fifteen hands high for a cavalry mount,' said Max Kerle knowingly.

'Sure — waal, I got some good ones right here. Them solids should sell. The mustangs are good, too — make good cowponies for the ranchers west of Delta . . . '

'Do I take it that just you and your daughter have driven these animals all that way?' inquired Stephen Crane pleasantly.

'Sure. Delia's as good as a man with a remuda.'

Stephen Crane bowed gallantly. His grey eyes swept appreciatively over the girl's figure. No one saw the cold, calculating look deep in his eyes. 'I'm sure she is very capable, Mr Breen. And very pretty, I am sure — if she was dressed in womanly clothes.'

'Delia don't worry none about clothes . . . ' said the mustanger. 'She's a good girl . . . '

'I am sure she is,' said Stephen Crane politely but his words were no indication of his grim thoughts. With a suddenness that was surely inspired by the devil, he knew that this young girl in the absurd clothes triggered off unspeakable desires in his harsh mind. There was a youthful quality, hidden in dusty jeans, shirt and ragged buckskin vest, that he wished he could possess. Of course, girls could be bought in certain wild towns across the territory, but they lacked this girl's freshness, a certain epitome of youth. The sudden wanting was something he had no intention of surpressing — a cold, cruel, arrogant lust!

'Howsabout selling us a horse, mister?' Max Kerle jerked. It was merely a play. He was waiting for some sign from Stephen Crane.

'Sure — why not, if we can agree on price?' said Walt Breen. 'Why don't we get down and light a fire and have a bite to eat and some coffee? I was just thinking about it — seein' the animals are nicely settled . . . '

And as if he was agreeable to the prospect of company, the man got down from his saddle. He walked about three yards, intending to go to the stack of provisions which had been dumped near the boulder.

Stephen Crane whipped out his Colt .45 and pointed it steadily at the mustanger. 'You, my man, are unfortunately in our way. I regret this but some of us are expendable.'

For a few seconds the mustanger froze, his hand a long way from his gun. 'Now, see here, mister, you ain't got no right — '

With cold-blooded deliberation Stephen Crane fired his gun. There was no attempt to give the other man a chance. The Colt roared death, a grim reflection on the real mentality of this callous man.

Walt Breen toppled slowly forward as hellish pain tore through him and whipped away in an instant the very core of his manhood. His knees buckled; he fell heavily to the earth and at the same time Delia's scream of shocked fear rang out.

The mustanger's horse jibbed in fright. The pack of horses wheeled a bit and Max Kerle and Kid Dawson, with quick reactions that were typical of their mode of living, went to pacify the herd, Kid Dawson sliding from Stephen Crane's horse and moving on foot.

At the same time, Delia crouched over her father's body. That he was dead there could be no doubt. Stephen Crane's gun had torn a hole in his heart. She leaned over the man who had been father and protector to her all her young life and cries of horror and anguish screamed from her throat.

Grinning evilly, Crane slid from his horse and walked closer to the girl. She rose like a fury and went for him with eye-gouging fingers. He had to use all his strength to beat her off. Then, with a quick thought, she dived to the boulder where lay the provisions.

Stephen Crane was no slouch where threats to his skin were concerned. He saw the signs. He saw the leather belt and the gun in the holster which was lying near the grubstake. So the girl wore a gun most of the time! A spirited filly, no less. But he would tame her.

His big strides took him to the boulder at the same time that the girl got there. He grabbed roughly at the gunbelt and pushed the girl to one side. She hit her head on the side of the boulder and lay for a few seconds as if dazed. The time element was enough for Stephen Crane to throw the gunbelt quickly to one side. When the girl recovered her wits, she saw this man crouching over her, his face a mask of harsh lust and cunning. Gone was the façade of the gentleman. In that moment Stephen Crane was revealed for what he was: an inhuman beast.

'Don't worry, my dear,' he sneered. 'You will be taken care of! I am a fine man — a person of some distinction — Stephen Crane is the name! You know, you are a very lovely girl — even in grief and with your face streaked in dust. There is something of the gamin in you . . . '

She clawed at him again, screaming abuse. 'You murderer! You dirty killer! Oh, my poor pa! You have killed him!'

He was holding her, enjoying in some cruel manner the way she fought him, when Max Kerle and Kid Dawson returned from calming the horses. They stood over Stephen Crane and the girl and laughed.

'Say, what d'you figure to do with her?' Kid Dawson guffawed. 'Looks like we'll have to kill her, too, Steve . . . '

Stephen Crane slapped the girl's face

in order to subdue her and then he rose to his feet. 'You are a fool, Dawson. And do not address me as Steve — unless you want me to break your neck! The girl will be protected — by me!'

'Protected!' Kid Dawson gaped. 'But — hell — we got plenty on our hands! We don't want a gal . . . '

'You sure oughta speak for yourself, Kid, boy,' mocked Max Kerle, with an admiring glance at the fair-haired girl. Her old stetson had fallen off. Her hair was a mass of corn-coloured curls, lovely enough to turn any man's head. Her womanly shape showed through the dusty check shirt. 'Seems like our colonel is mighty attracted to this bit of female — and I can't say I rightly blame him — except our colonel is just a bit too long in the tooth for this little filly but never mind . . . '

He got a hard stare from Stephen Crane for his taunts, but that did not worry Max Kerle. He had his secret thoughts, too. He did not bawl out the first things that came into his head, like Kid Dawson.

There was the gold; a two-way share was better than three. But better still if it went the way of only one man!

Then there was the pack of horse-flesh. Sure, it was worth dinero in the right quarter, but fifty animals needed handling all the way to Delta. Too many for one man!

And now a girl! She wasn't worth money, but pleasures always cost a price! It had been a long time since he'd had a woman. This Delia Breen looked a real peacheroo! Still, Stephen Crane had the same thoughts!

'We don't need the gal!' yelled Kid Dawson. 'Heck, we gotta look in at the mine at Yellow Stones! And hows about pushin' on for Gallery?'

'He'll keep, you dumb fool!' rapped Max Kerle.

'How you goin' to explain this gal when we hit Delta?' raged the Kid.

'Let me take care of that,' said Stephen Crane coldly. 'This girl will go along with us — for the time being.'

'Aw, I get you! Just for the time being . . . '

'How far are we from this Yellow Stones area, Dawson?' Stephen Crane rapped with his old authority.

'Sure, ain't far . . . just a few miles . . . I'll know the place soon as I get near it . . . '

'We'll drive the horses over there. We might be able to find a rough corral among the rocks — if the terrain is as broken as you say, Dawson.'

'It's sure rough. Big rocks standin' like barns and gullies — all this yellow stone — sandstone, I guess.'

'Then we corral the horses and look into this question of further gold. That won't take long.'

'You figure to plug the old galoot and his daughter when we get there?' sneered Max Kerle. 'Not that it throws me, *amigo* . . . '

'If we need to.'

'And you'll corral that gal, too!' Max Kerle laughed harshly. 'By God, Crane, you got an appetite!'

'For the good things in life, you mean?' Stephen Crane ran his eyes over the crying girl again. 'Yes, there are certain lusts in a man — the need for money, women, drink, a good hand of cards. I admit to liking all these carnal pleasures . . . '

'And, boy, how you talk!' sneered the other. 'Just like as if we was all some dirt under them boots, huh, Crane?'

'Don't attempt to be clever, Kerle . . . '

Max Kerle turned away. 'We've got a pack of work to do. Hope you aim to do your share of it, Crane.'

'Look, Mr Crane,' blustered the Kid, 'leave that gal — or shoot her — 'cause sure as hell she'll be trouble!'

'You will obey me, Dawson.'

The command had all the breed of authority, and left Kid Dawson staring and blustering. But the time for word-play was over because there was work to do. Delia Breen backed to the boulder, wishing she could kill this tall, hateful man with the greying hair and moustache, while the other two men saw to their mounts. Kid Dawson took the mustanger's saddled animal; jerked at the leathers to assure himself everything was okay; held the head harness. Max Kerle circled the group of horses, noting appreciatively their good qualities. This string of broom-tails was worth money, especially in Delta where the army was buying, if the rumours were correct. He came right back to where Crane was standing, watching the girl, a nasty twist on his lips.

'We're ready to go,' said Max Kerle.

'She's got a mount hidden in the shade of that big rock,' said the other. 'Watch her while I secure the animal . . . '

Crane strode off. The girl eyed Kerle as if she wished him dead. Then she began to move slowly.

'You ain't goin' anywhere, missy.' Kerle's voice was a mere warning.

'Am I not allowed to walk . . . ?'

'All right.' He grinned. 'Walk. You look good walkin'!'

She moved slowly, uncertainly around him, and he watched her, amused. There was some wild grace in her limbs . . . Crane was right . . . she had style . . .

And then she dived like a wild thing for her father's body — and the gun still stuck in his holster.

Max Kerle was really late in starting his reaction, and as he dived at her, she whipped the gun out. She was slick with a Colt even though the weapon looked like a small cannon in her hand. The gun roared and flashed almost in Max Kerle's face. He felt the hiss of the slug as it cut air only inches from his head. And then he was struggling with the girl, grabbing at the gun and wrenching it from her grasp. He flung it away. She made an instinctive attempt to dive after it. He grabbed her, held her in a vicious hug that nearly cracked her ribs. For some seconds she stared into his furious, dirty, bewhiskered face, glaring back defiantly at him. Then as he knew he had bested the girl, he kept her in the tight embrace and chuckled triumphantly while she regarded him with loathing.

'Let me go! You — killer — you — '

'Wall, now, I'm right happy just holdin' you, Miss Delia Breen . . . '

'Get your stinking hands off her!' The grating command right behind him held no humour. Max Kerle looked up to see the hard angry expression on Stephen Crane's face.

'Why, this little gal tried to kill me! Just went for her old pa's gun — and I was mighty lucky to dodge that slug. Yessir!'

A hand like a vice descended on Kerle's shoulder and rammed him back. The girl pushed free. She watched as Max Kerle faced the man who considered himself superior.

'You sore about somethin'?'

Max Kerle's sneer was an insult in itself. 'You figure to take all the cake — Colonel — sir . . . '

'Leave — her — alone!' The hissed command was full of real menace. 'That's an order. I mean it, Kerle.'

Kid Dawson watched the other two men with a kind of stupid irritation. He had a one-track mind; the chores that lay ahead nagged at him; this girl was a complete nuisance.

'Are you two out of your minds?' he barked. His full face was creased in anger. 'I've a doggone mind to take my share of the gold and light out for Gallery on my own!'

'You do, Kid, old boy,' taunted Max Kerle. 'You go right ahead — ask the general for your share. You do that, boy!'

But there was only muttered comments at that suggestion, and the three men turned to the horses. Crane had brought the girl's small mare from the nook where it had been tethered. He then told Kerle to tie the girl's hands together in front of her while he held her shoulders. She begged them to bury her father, but her pleas were callously ignored. Sobbing, helpless, she was overpowered, then forced to vault to her saddle. Stephen Crane fashioned a lead rope from the coil which was looped on his horse and tied one end to the leathers of the small mare. Then he got up to his saddle, watching her with a cold smile.

Kid Dawson, under instruction, took as much of the grubstake which had belonged to the mustanger as he could tie around his newly acquired mount. Then he and Max Kerle rode out wide to circle the pack of horses while Stephen Crane, with the girl's mount on the lead rope, rode drag. In this manner, they got the herd moving, slowly because they did not want to spook them.

After some miles, when they were used to the pack and the vagaries of about two horses in particular, they were moving nicely. Walking horses moved faster than a cattle herd. They made good progress, and then Kid

Dawson gave a shout and pointed to the near horizon.

'That's the Yellow Stones! Always figured they was just rock and cactus — a hideout for sidewinders. I ain't never moseyed into 'em.'

'Waal, we aim to this time,' said Max Kerle. 'Maybe there's some more gold . . . '

The pile-up of rocks lay like a yellowish tinge on the skyline, becoming larger and more definite as they drove the horses over the undulating, chaparral-studded land. When they got real close to the weathered stands of rock, they looked like a natural corral. In a place like this there was nearly always a blind canyon or a basin where animals could be herded. They found a large recess which took the pack. They rolled some boulders closer together. Kid Dawson elected to stand guard while the other two rode into the Yellow Stones.

They had been gone about half an hour, and he was cursing the heat and brooding about Jim Gallery, when he was startled by a flurry of gunshots. The sounds came from inside the rocky maze! Had Crane and Kerle killed the other man and girl?

6

Colt Shindig

Jim Gallery watched the figure of Mack Slater ride up and halt his elderly horse. The man pushed back his hat and used his red bandanna to mop his brow. 'Sure is plenty hot among these rocks!' he said cheerfully.

Jim Gallery waited. He noted the appraisal which the sheriff gave him. Then it came. 'I've seen you in Delta, mister . . . '

'I've been there,' admitted Jim.

'What brings you out here, Sheriff?' Helen Mackay asked.

'Two wanderin' hellions, Miss Mackay.' He smiled. 'You know a lawman hears more in the saloons than he'll ever get handed to him if he tramped the town askin' questions day and night! Now I heard some darned disturbin' news last night. Seems two hardcases came out this way to look for gold — your gold, miss. Oh, sure, folks in Delta know your dad struck a nice little find out here . . . '

'You are too late,' said Helen bitterly. 'Two men did ride in here last night. They stole all the gold my father has worked for over the months and even shot him . . . '

'Shot him? Is he bad?'

'Not too ill. This man — Jim Gallery — was camped on the trail and he helped me. My father was bleeding badly from the wound . . . '

'You were near here last night?' Mack Slater turned shrewd eyes on Jim Gallery. He sat hunched, easy in his saddle, his thumbs hooked into his belt, his clean tan shirt bulging a little across a generous stomach. 'You like spendin' the nights in these wild parts, *amigo*?'

'Nope. I like towns,' Jim Gallery smiled back. 'I like food that some other galoot has cooked and I like a nice chintz table-cloth.'

'Some feller hit you lately?'

'A man in Delta . . . '

'Fightin' don't do a man much good!' The sheriff shook his head sadly. 'In Delta you say?'

'Yep . . . '

'Funny,' said Mack Slater, 'when I saw you ride out you sure looked mighty handsome. None of them bruises under your eyes. And you were ridin' a different horse . . . I was watching you. You weren't in Delta for any kind of work or business . . . '

'You must get a few drifters in your town,' drawled Jim.

Mack Slater nodded. 'Waal, it don't signify none. You want me to take a look at your pa, Miss Mackay? I know plenty about wounds.'

'Well, a second opinion might be a good idea. And my father likes you — he'd love to talk . . . '

'I'll ride back with you, Helen,' said Jim Gallery quietly. 'Then — maybe when the sheriff is set to return to Delta, I'll go with him. Mighty good thing to have the law ride with you!'

In actual fact, Helen prepared a meal for the sheriff and he helped himself to coffee. Bert Mackay walked stiffly into the room and seemed eager to talk with the sheriff. Jim Gallery settled back, watching Helen, thinking that this young woman was a real beauty. Was he being too impressed? If she knew the truth about him ... knew about the Drago Cattlemen's Bank robbery, for instance ... Well, a man should not dwell on the grim facts of life.

'They was two damned town scum!' snapped Bert Mackay. 'They came bustin' in and demanded gold. The skunks shot me — just to prove they weren't foolin'!'

'Not those two,' remarked Mack Slater. 'You were dealing with two hell-bents. They're not really Delta men — just scum that drifted in, as you say ... '

'I hope that gold is a curse to 'em!' roared Bert. 'Damn their hides! If I was fit I'd ride out after 'em.'

'I'll ride around — but they'll be headin' for freedom in any direction by now. Waal, this is mighty nice apple pie, Miss Helen.' Mack Slater licked his lips. 'I'll put out Wanted posters for them two gents that robbed you, Bert — not that there's much chance of finding them. They'll hightail it for some out-of-the-way place where they can sell the gold . . . '

'Damn them! I've a good mind to ride out . . . '

'You're not fit, Mr Mackay,' said Jim Gallery quietly. 'That wound wouldn't allow you to get far . . . '

'Father — you can't ride out!' protested Helen.

'I'll mosey around,' said Mack Slater, 'but I can't travel far. There's things to take care of in town. Judge Petter is holdin' a court tomorrow and I got to be there — and I got two drunks in the cells . . . '

'Thanks for riding out to warn us,' said the girl, 'but it's too late, of course.'

The sheriff rose to go, refreshed after the coffee and the food. Jim Gallery went with him to the tierail outside. They mounted the horses; spent a few minutes talking to Helen and Bert Mackay and then left, moving along the rocky defile that led out of the Yellow Stones. The last Jim Gallery saw of the girl, she was waving goodbye to him. He twisted back in his saddle, a tinge of regret in his mind. Well, maybe he would return . . .

He had Harry Carslake on his mind — and the three hellions he had left way back in the area near the old Indian well. That they would trail him — or at least reach Delta — he had no doubt. They had guns, food and water — and legs — and they were experienced travellers! Sure, they'd hit Delta . . .

'You just rode out here, young feller, and camped somewheres out in the open — and then Miss Mackay found you?' Mack Slater asked suddenly.

'That's the way of it . . . '

'Ain't much reason,' said the sheriff shrewdly. 'And you ain't totin' a gun. Now when you left Delta you was all fixed up with Colt and rifle . . . '

'I know — you saw me!'

'Sure thing. That's the way I do things. I just mosey around . . . '

Jim Gallery smiled thinly. He would put up with the middle-aged sheriff's rumbling comments, his attempts to pump him until they reached town and then, after trading this horse for another animal, and buying some new gear, he'd ride out on the long search for Harry Carslake and the missing money. For that little investigation he'd need guns.

They rode through twisting gullies, where tall rocks stood up on all sides like jagged teeth and the green cholla cactus filled many a hole and crevice. They had nearly reached the open land when they suddenly spotted the approaching two horses and riders. The recognition was mutual — on Jim Gallery's side!

Stephen Crane and Max Kerle! Mounted! How the hell had they managed that?

A big hunk of rock, standing like a crazy monument that had been fashioned by wind and rain, was nearby. Jim Gallery jigged his horse immediately into the cover. 'In here, Sheriff! Them *hombres* . . . '

He was too late. A hail of fire spurted from the guns of the two approaching riders and Mack Slater was caught in it. A slug tore into his chest, jerking him back on the saddle. Another made a bloody hole in his forehead. The onslaught tore the life out of him and he began to topple as his horse jigged and pranced in fright.

Jim Gallery was in the cover afforded by the fantastically shaped spire of rock. As Mack Slater hit the ground, he dashed out, grabbed the body and dragged him to the rock. The sheriff was obviously dead, a flashing glance was all that was needed to check that. Jim took the man's Colt. He crouched.

He whipped a glance at the horse as it slewed in a futile, prancing circle. The animal came closer to where Jim Gallery crouched, gun in hand, the other hand holding his own animal's leathers. It was fairly near, and he thought the rifle in the saddle holster would be a good thing! If he could get it!

He darted for the animal, thinking to get the rifle before the horse veered away again. As he came out in the open, more slugs from hand guns spat furiously at him and kicked up dust and rock chips — but not one hit him! He tugged at the rifle, hastily grabbed at the horse's trailing reins and then dived back for cover. The animal came willingly with him. He looped the leathers around a jagged outcrop of rock; attended to his own horse in the same fashion and then took a swift scrutiny of his surroundings.

He was all right — as long as Crane and Kerle stayed where they were in the defile. But if they figured to climb the nearby tall rocks they could get above him and, indeed, circle him. Two men could always cook up an advantage over one!

He did not spend much time wondering how they had got mounts. He had seen that they were not the horses he had driven off miles from the Indian well.

Jim Gallery edged to the corner of the rock; tried a couple of shots in the general direction of the two men and then desisted. He would have to conserve his ammunition. He couldn't reload. He had no spare slugs. Probably the rifle was fully loaded.

If he could kill Stephen Crane and Max Kerle in this little ruckus it would not cause him the slightest regret.

It wasn't entirely unexpected when he heard raging remarks from the two men. 'You — Gallery — so this is where you got to!' It was Max Kerle, full of fury. 'You're one tricky *hombre* — but we'll leave you for buzzard bait this time!'

Jim Gallery decided to benefit from an exchange of shouts. 'How did you know I was here?'

'We didn't!' came Stephen Crane's cool retort. 'We rode in here for other reasons — but we're certainly glad to catch up with you. It couldn't be better. We have the advantage, Gallery — two to one! We'll kill you this time.'

'You know what you've done,' yelled Jim. 'You've shot the sheriff from Delta. He's dead!'

'Now ain't that too bad!' came Max Kerle's sneering shout.

'He was respected in town. The folks back there don't like killers.'

'Gallery, you know we don't give a damn,' shouted Stephen Crane contemptuously. 'We're going to kill you, too. I dislike you more than ever. You have repeatedly tried to best me. First by handing me over for bounty money and then tricking us at the Indian well. Kerle has his reasons for hating you — mainly money.'

'Aw, the hell with this yap!' The

hoarse yell tore from Max Kerle. 'Let's kill him. That's what we want — and then we got other things to do!'

Jim Gallery wondered where Kid Dawson was placed. Was he with them? Strange that he should be silent! No — the Kid must be elsewhere. Probably at the mouth of the Yellow Stones. Maybe keeping a lookout.

He knew he had to get above the other two men before they did the same to him. With a quick look around, he leaped for a rising hillock of sand, shale and cactus that rose just to his left. At the top of the hillock a pinnacle of rock stood like a giant's tooth. It would be a good vantage point.

As he moved shots barked at him and came grimly near, digging into the ground all around him, but he was leaping, moving like a frantic animal and he was a difficult target. He jumped to a boulder, rested a moment and then darted lithely to another. The last part was the most dangerous; he had to race up a shale slope where there was no cover. He attracted a hail of bullets. Someone was using a rifle, too, and that he did not like. He dug his heels into the soft slope, sending shale slithering down, and he darted like mad for the pinnacle.

He reached cover, hugged the rock for some moments and then sighted his rifle. It was good to have the feel of a gun again. He saw the black shape of Max Kerle down below, just to one side of a big outcrop of rock. He fired, two quick shots. He missed the man and swore because this was not some fool game. He wanted to kill. Max Kerle dived for new cover, yelling furiously, his cries echoing in the defile.

Jim Gallery bit his lip. He was short of ammunition. Sure, he had the guns — but no spare slugs. He'd have to watch it. If the other two realised his shortage, they would play with him, make him waste shots. Well, there was only one answer: he'd have to get in a killer shot — or at least wound a man. But they wouldn't scare easily . . .

Down in the defile Max Kerle rapped across to Stephen Crane, 'He's above us — the tricky swine. Moved fast! Now why'n hell did he stop by in this place, huh?'

'Maybe figured it for a hideout instead of Delta . . . ' Momentarily, Stephen Crane used the western lingo he so often effected to despise.

'We'll have to move out — get around him,' muttered Max Kerle. 'Say, that was a lawman we killed!'

'Does that matter?' came the other man's cool tones.

Max Kerle was thinking: somebody might get killed here! And just when there's gold a-plenty! Hell, it made a man think! Sure, he hated Jim Gallery — but as Crane had said it was all dinero. There had been the suspicion that Gallery had done him out of the Drago loot by some strange means, but proof had been sadly lacking.

A man didn't want to die when he had his hands on gold. A man didn't want to die at any time, except that there were things he had to face up to, insults and grievances he wouldn't swallow.

Now if Crane got himself killed trying to buzzard-bait Gallery no one would lose much sleep. With Crane out of the way, the gold would go much further. Even the mob of horses could be handled by the Kid and himself.

'Are we goin' to move out and get that jigger?' Max Kerle asked. He watched the other man furtively. Would Crane take chances and stop a slug? Or was it best to successfully polish off Gallery and stick with his partner — until the gold was ready to be shared?

'Move around him,' muttered Stephen Crane. 'Use the rifles! All we need is one good shot and that saddletramp will be out of our hair!'

Leaving the horses tied in a rocky nook, the two men separated and began climbing carefully among the debris of rocks that littered this broken land. They hoped to get the edge on Gallery;

get around him and get a glimpse of him for just long enough to snap off a fast accurate shot.

Max Kerle looked backwards, sombrely, at the horses — and the significant little sacks of gold tied around the saddles. There was real spending money there which was readily exchangeable in any frontier town for the good things of life — drink, gambling and a woman!

He looked carefully ahead, at the slope of shale and the pinnacle of rock which sheltered Gallery. The tricky devil was lying low, pretty silent.

'Waitin', huh!' muttered Max Kerle. 'Or maybe he ain't got too much lead left for them smoke-poles . . .

He crawled around a boulder and then decided to dart to another. As he darted forward, hunched, his dirty boots scuffing into the loose soil, Jim Gallery spotted him and chanced two shots. Max Kerle swore viciously as the bullets stung the ground close to him, and his last movement was a desperate dive to the boulder, where he lay dragging in breath, his face close to warm rock. The gritty dust stuck to the saliva on his lips. His fingers gripped the rifle tightly with rage.

'Damn you, Gallery! I'll get you . . . '

Stephen Crane was taking a wide loop that would bring him up behind Jim Gallery, so that the lean man would have to contend with fire from two directions. Stephen Crane's movements took time to accomplish, but that was an essential of good tactics. He made a difficult climb up some ledges of rock which made him pant a bit, but then he was ready. Gallery was below him, hugging the tooth-like pinnacle, watching Max Kerle. Stephen Crane raised his rifle. He was an excellent shot, army trained in the use of firearms and accurate when he had time to aim.

He sighted deliberately, sure that he would kill Jim Gallery. He wasn't going to miss. This was the end of the annoying swine . . .

Crack — Crack!

The second shot was delayed and almost unnecessary. Jim Gallery jerked like some animal impaled by an agonising knife and then fell face forward and lay still.

Stephen Crane could not resist an exultant shout. 'Got him!' And then he stood up, waving his gun.

Max Kerle rose from the boulder which was sheltering him as if he was some kind of ground rat. He stood up and yelled back at his partner. 'You sure? You gutted the rannigan?'

'I got him . . . '

'Yippee! Ain't that the good news! Say, let's take a look . . . '

'If you want to,' shouted Stephen Crane.

Both men began to converge on the tall pinnacle of rock at the base of which lay Jim Gallery's prone body.

They were out in the open, boots digging roughly into the loose earth as they climbed the slope, when the deep bark of rifles sounded behind them and bullets hissed angrily around them. The two men leaped for cover. More shots spat into the ground close to them.

Away down the defile, on a flat shelf of rock, Helen Mackay and her father stood openly and pumped shell after shell at the two men.

'Let's get!' yelled Max Kerle. 'I aim to live — and spend that gold! We got Gallery — that's all that matters!'

7

A Double-Crossing Gent

They rode dangerously out of the broken, rocky land, urging the horses in a way that could have snapped a leg in two if the animals had put a wrong foot forward. But with the luck of their kind the snorting mounts reached the sandy defile that led to the end of the rocky outcrops, and then they were near to the rough corral where the horses cropped at the sparse grass and Kid Dawson waited, expectant, gun at the ready. The blonde girl was dumped in a corner among sun-bleached rocks and Kid Dawson had tied a big square slab of sandstone to a length of rope which in turn was looped around her wrists. She could not run far with this anchor.

'What in hell was all that shootin'?'

rapped the Kid.

'We got Gallery!'

'Dead?'

'I sighted on him,' said Stephen Crane coolly, 'and he'll be dead!' It was an arrogant assertion, befitting his character and intended to sneer at the younger man.

'Wha — what was Gallery doin' here?'

'We rode right into him — and the blamed sheriff from Delta. We cut the lawman down right away . . . '

'Waal, ain't that somethin'!' The Kid stood with his mouth agape. Then he returned stubbornly to the main point. 'What in tarnation was Gallery doin' in this pile of rocks?'

'Must've figured it for a hideout,' said Max Kerle.

Stephen Crane rubbed his unshaven jaw. 'Now why did the sheriff visit this place? Rather strange! It isn't possible they contacted the sheriff so quickly about their loss of the gold! Hmm — well, it doesn't really matter.' He turned eyes that suddenly gleamed to the golden-haired girl and walked closer to her, sudden, smouldering ideas crowding into his brain. 'Ah, how is my dear little girl . . . ?'

When he got too close she kicked out at him and, in fact, rammed a boot against his shin. With an angry hiss of breath Stephen Crane raised a warning hand, as if to strike her. 'You'll pay for that, my dear, when I feel like dealing with you!'

'You dirty ruffian!' cried the girl. 'I'll kill you! You stinkin', inhuman brute! You killed my dear old pa . . . '

But the tall, older man just walked away, smiling grimly — though her words rankled in the mind of a man who had once commanded respect and worn the uniform of a famous regiment. He would have revenge!

'Now, look here,' argued Kid Dawson, 'I don't get all that shootin'. You came ridin' out like there was Apaches on your trail!'

'If we must spell it out,' sneered

Stephen Crane, 'we ran into the old prospector and his daughter. I saw them — damned well pumping rifle shots at us. Seems to me they were friendly with Gallery; Well, they can bury him!'

That remark brought a guffaw of delight from Max Kerle. For the time being the relationship between the partners in killing was amicable.

'Are we hightailin' it to Delta with these horses now that we've done with Gallery?'

'That's the idea,' said Kerle. 'I say we forget about any gold in this place — for the time being. We got plenty to do.'

'We can always come back,' rejoined Stephen Crane. 'At some future date, my friends. When we have had our pleasures . . . ' And he threw another glance at Delia Breen as she hugged the rock face and glared at them. 'Perhaps by that time these simple-minded mining people will have won some more gold. I have a feeling that those two ruffians took all there was, in any case.'

'And now we got it,' stated Kid Dawson. He grinned at the others, his round face pudgy and slightly stupid. 'I feel good, Steve! Gallery dead — wish I'd done it — and gold for the spendin'! Ain't it good, Max?'

He did not notice the scowl that Stephen Crane handed him. And he certainly could not read his mind. Stephen Crane was thinking: you scruffy, low-class range rat! If you make such familiar use of my name again, I'll shoot you where you stand! I will not tolerate an upstart!

'How about chow?' questioned Max Kerle. 'I need grub. Wish I had some whisky . . . or even tequila with a pinch of salt!'

'You figure the prospector and his gal will come after us?' asked the Kid.

'Don't be stupid!' The hawk-like man could not resist the dig. 'A gal — and an oldster!'

'They made you ride like hell . . . '

'There won't be a second time! Say, let's have some blasted coffee. Light a fire, Kid. I'm sick of drinkin' water . . . '

Without any qualms about the killings they had behind them, the three men busied themselves with the chores. Food was prepared, rustled from the stores belonging to the mustanger. There was soon the sizzling sound of sidemeat frying in a pan and coffee bubbling in a pot.

The girl backed to the rock face and watched them, a trifle fearfully, because she saw the terrible truth stamped on the faces of these men. They were killers, knowing nothing of mercy.

'Well, if we want to reach civilisation and enjoy some refined living, we've got work to do,' stated Stephen Crane. 'If we drive we can be in Delta by nightfall — despite this heat.'

'And the horses?'

'We'll sell them quickly. We may want to get out of town fast. Gold can be taken anywhere . . . '

'And this gal?' Kid Dawson jerked a

thumb at her. 'You aim to take her into town? She'll screech like a night-owl . . . '

'I won't be such a fool as to take her into town,' countered the other. 'I have a better idea. Just outside of Delta I've noticed an old deserted shack near the ruined mission. I'll push the girl in there until I can return — and then — '

'Yeah?' Max Kerle jeered. 'This filly sure has you goin', Crane! You figure you can handle her? Maybe you need help . . . '

'We'll share the gold — nothing else!'

The urgency of the work ahead was very real if they wanted to reach Delta by nightfall.

★ ★ ★

Two miles out of the town the old ruined mission stood, its crumbling walls a monument to the old padres who had travelled up from across the Rio Grande to found a chain of missions. But the Apaches had also moved north, on frequent raids, and they had wiped out the padres and burned the roof for the last time. The place had never been repaired. Some old sourdough had built a shack nearby — and it was to this crude shelter that Stephen Crane took the girl. He pushed her into the place, alone, the horses somewhere down the slope, near the cottonwoods, attended by Max Kerle and Kid Dawson.

'You will stay here,' said the man cruelly. 'I'll return, when I have more time. There's no need for fear, my girl — I am quite capable of treating you like a lady, if you will allow me . . . '

'I hate you!'

'Well, that emotion will suffice for a start!' mocked the other.

Her hands were still tied. He had rope and so he forced her to sit down and submit to being roped to an old, rough chair. 'You will stay here — for the night. Maybe I'll come out to see you — but perhaps I'll be too drunk even to appreciate your loveliness.'

'You're a monster!' breathed the girl. 'I swear I'll kill you . . . '

'How? With your hands?' His eyes gleamed. 'That might be an interesting scuffle — and I am so much stronger than you.' He lightly touched her hair; then ran a hand down her arm. 'Ah — youth — a pity you can't willingly come to me — but perhaps in my more genial moments I might try to win you over . . . '

'You're a brute!'

'Just a harsh man,' he said grimly. 'You'll learn in the next day or two. And now I must go. My low companions insist we get to town. We need to get rid of fifty horses . . . quickly . . . '

And that was true. The pack of horses, although representing a useful sum of money, were beginning to assume a nuisance value because they needed time and attention. Fifty animals had to be constantly watched and there were two lead mares that seemed to be imbued with an itch to wander off. Kid Dawson had cursed them repeatedly and rounded them back into the pack.

When Stephen Crane returned to the other two men, there were some snarled comments about the delay. 'Hey, when are we going to hit town and get rid of these broomtails, Crane?'

'All right — push on!' rapped the other. 'We'll find corral space to hire somewhere in town even if we don't actually make a deal tonight. Might be better that way. We'll haggle with the army agents in our own time.'

'Waal, the sheriff is dead,' joked Max Kerle. 'Ain't no one to ask nosy questions. Gallery is dead — we don't have to worry about him. Same goes for the mustanger — he can't argue. And them two bad *hombres* who so kindly lifted the gold, for us — why, those two galoots are plumb dead, too! Just seems like we got everythin' goin' our way, Crane, old man, Colonel — sir . . . '

Stephen Crane's eyes glinted at the sheer insolence displayed by this drifter. Kerle had better watch his tongue and his manners. A Colt slug could even up faster than a bolt of lightning; the solid little bags of gold were a big inducement to this end!

The plan worked out fine for the three killers. They found a corral and the man who owned it, and agreed to pay his price for the night's hire. The horses were driven into the poles and the gate made fast. As the animals swirled around the confines, Max Kerle said, 'Waal, that little chore is done! How about a drink?'

'When do we share the gold?' demanded Kid Dawson. He jigged his horse — close to the other men. 'I reckon it's time . . . '

'We need two more canvas sacks,' said Stephen Crane smoothly, 'and then we can share the gold out into six pokes — making two for each man. Ideally, we should weigh the stuff.'

'Rough and ready will do for me,' grunted the Kid.

'How about gettin' us a room at a hotel,' suggested Max Kerle, 'and then we could stash the gold for the night. We can sell it tomorrow. There's an assayer's office in town. They might buy it — or the bank. It's easier to share out real dinero . . . '

'You are coming up with remarkably acute ideas, Kerle,' said Stephen Crane. 'I'm in favour of the hotel room and a neat hiding place for the gold until tomorrow. Then we'll sell. Dollar bills look good. We can collect on the horses, too . . . '

'Right — share-out tomorrow,' snapped Kid Dawson. 'Maybe it is too late to sell the gold tonight . . . '

'Not too late for a damned good drink!' gloated Max Kerle.

They booked into a room at a cheap hotel, leaving their horses with a liveryman and tramping up the stairs of the hotel with heavy, tired limbs. It had been a long day. They needed relaxation. The gold was taken with them, along with their saddlebags and guns. It was typical of Stephen Crane that while the other two merely beat dust out of their clothes and went hurriedly to the nearest saloon, he sent for warm water. He washed, shaved and brought out a clean checked shirt from his saddle-bag. When he joined the other two in the saloon, he looked at least present-able.

They had some ready cash and could buy drinks. The saloon was full, a card game going solidly at one table; two white-aproned bartenders supply-ing bottles and glasses behind a bar; two girls in off-shouldered dresses were perched on the laps of two big rannigans who were immaculate in narrow-lapelled store suits.

'We're sittin' pretty,' chuckled Max Kerle. 'Gold — and Gallery dead!'

'I hope you are not intending to shout these facts from the bar-top,' said Stephen Crane coldly.

'What the hell! Crane — just cut out that goddamn uppity way of talkin'! We've had a bellyful! I say we're sittin' pretty — and I don't want to listen to you tellin' me what to do!'

'You'll end up drunk.'

'Waal, ain't that great! I'd like to get drunk — you hear! I reckon what we done deserves a few drinks — ain't that right, Kid, *amigo*? Ain't we done well?'

'Pretty good.' Kid Dawson nodded foolishly. Already he had downed three shots of whisky. It was, admittedly, poor stuff and produced by some enterprising still owner in Kansas. 'Yeah, we done got rid of Gallery . . . the polecat . . . wish I'd filled him with lead . . . '

'And we got gold!' yelled Max Kerle. 'Yes, sirree, we got enough gold to buy this goddamn bar!'

A lantern-jawed rangehand standing near to Max Kerle pricked up his ears at the mention of the word. Max Kerle gulped again at his glass and reached for the bottle of golden liquid.

Stephen Crane endured another ten minutes of the foolish banter between the two men, and then decided that fools drank while other men acted. The time had arrived for him to shake off these two uncouth louts, and what better if a man rode out with more than his share of gold! It was there, for the taking, in the hotel room, and he had the key, being the last to leave. He didn't need to get drunk; that state of idiocy could always come later.

He sidled away and made for the batwings. He went out into the night where yellow lanterns gleamed at infrequent intervals down the main stem. Some passing men tramped along the board walk. Further along the street, light spilled from another saloon and he heard the clanging of an aged piano hammered out by some heavy-handed musician.

If Max Kerle and the Kid got drunk, half the men in the bar would know about the gold by midnight — and that would be dangerous.

He took big strides back down the main stem. He paused at the corral where the fifty head stood patiently. On an impulse, he lifted the retaining pole and moved into the corral. He selected a big black and a smaller mustang that looked obedient. He led them out, holding the manes. He slid the pole back, locking the gate.

He led the two animals along to the livery and got the hostler to saddle the black with his own saddle and provide another rig for the small mustang. The two animals were brought along to the tierail outside the hotel. Stephen Crane went into the building and ten minutes later came out with the four bags of gold, guns and his saddlebags.

8

Survive — or Die

They lifted him up and carried the limp body back to the cabin in the rocky gulch, a trail of blood marking their passage. Old Bert Mackay could use only one arm, and even that effort pulled muscles which gave him much pain, and he had to carry his rifle at the same time. So the bulk of the man's weight fell on Helen. She supported his shoulders and had to stop frequently. Each time they rested she noted the eyes closed in unconsciousness or death and this created a desperate fear in her heart. Oh, of all the futile waste!

Helen and her father had heard the gunshots soon after Jim had left with the sheriff. Fearfully, they had run out, armed. Bert Mackay had insisted upon accompanying his daughter. It was just as well that two rifles had spoken instead of one. The two men had spurred their horses and escaped down the defile.

In the house she bent over Jim. Her father brought water and a cloth which she used on Jim's head. Blood had matted into his hair and painted his face fearfully, like a mask. But when she wiped the blood away, he looked a lot better except for the terrible, long red wound right down the side of his head, just above the ear.

She slid a hand to his heart; paused and then thrilled with a new hope.

'He isn't dead, Pa. He's alive . . . '

The old man nodded wisely. 'A crease! He's missed death by an inch, daughter! He'll come round — maybe soon — maybe later — and he'll have a mighty sore head. And hair will never grow on that scar again!'

'He's got to live!' breathed the girl.

'I reckon he will,' said the oldster. 'He's a hard galoot . . . '

But Jim Gallery stayed unconscious

for hours, concussed by the one shot that had found him. Stephen Crane had nearly accomplished his murderous intent, but not quite. His aim had been accurate — but maybe Jim Gallery had moved slightly. In a shooting match these things happened — and it had saved a life.

She could not leave his side; staring down at this rock-hard man, noting his deep breathing. With his eyes closed the lean imprint of his face was accentuated. He had shaved earlier that day but there was still a blue shadow around his chin. Something in his present helplessness made her stretch out a hand to lightly touch his brow. Her father, walking stiffly into the room at that moment, saw the gesture and smiled faintly. The way of a woman with a man to nurse!

'I'll have to get the sheriff's body back here,' muttered Bert Mackay. 'Can you help me, gal? I can't leave him out there . . .'

'Those gunslingers!' Anger flushed

Helen's face. 'Why did they have to kill Mack Slater? Who are they? Why did they come here?'

'Looks to me like they've been trailin' this man, honey,' and the oldster indicated Jim Gallery.

'Why?' She paused. 'What did he do to them?'

'Maybe we'll know pretty soon . . . '

They went out to deal with the sheriff's body, finding it another hard, distasteful chore. But Mack Slater had always been friendly with Bart Mackay and they had to do something respectful for the body.

'I'll make a cairn over the body — way down in the sandy draw,' said the old man.

When Helen Mackay got back to the cabin and leaned anxiously over Jim Gallery again, she saw his eyes move, momentarily it was true, but this was a sign of returning consciousness. From then on she was in a state of excitement, watching him, leaning over him, cleaning his face again. Then she made soup, thinking he might need something reviving and nourishing.

By the time the sun was sinking way out on the rim of the badland areas, Jim Gallery was back in the world. His eyes followed the girl dazedly. He lay back on the bunk and when he tried to move she insisted that he lie still.

'You've been badly hurt. You must rest — Jim . . . '

'Wha — wha — what happened to me?'

She did not burden him with a long-winded rigmarole. She simply said, 'You were creased — but you'll be all right. Just lie still . . . would you like some soup?'

He tried to grin but that brought shooting pains down one side of his face. He watched her as she busied herself around the cabin. She came with a bowl of the soup and insisted that he drink it. She fed him with a large spoon.

An hour later, when the sun had disappeared and some lone coyote howled from some lofty perch, he sat up despite her attempts to make him lie still. 'You're like an old hen,' he said gruffly. Then, gently, 'Thanks, Helen. It's good . . . to have . . . someone fuss a bit. But I'll be all right. I remember everything now . . . '

'Two men shot at you . . . '

'Yep. Two killers — Stephen Crane and Max Kerte . . . '

'Who are they? What did they want?'

'Me, mostly — dead.'

'What a grim thing to say! Why, Jim — why?'

'It's a kinda long story,' he sighed. 'And you wouldn't appreciate most of it. It ain't the thing a woman would like . . . '

'I'd like to know more about these men,' she said spiritedly.

'Well, there's three . . . another feller called Kid Dawson . . . all dangerous . . . when you found me without boots and guns I'd just gotten away from them. They want me dead. I left them without horses — after they'd left me to drown — it's a boring account, Helen! One thing puzzles me — and that's how come they rode into the Yellow Stones. How did they know I was here? Tracked? But they ain't so hot at that little Injun trick — I know that for sure!'

'Well, they rode away when pa and I fired at them. They left you for dead. I'm sure they figure you're dead . . . '

'They are goin' to get one heck of a surprise,' said Jim Gallery grimly, and he sat up. She protested and he said harshly, 'I'm getting on my feet, Helen. Don't try to stop me.'

'You've got a raw wound along your head . . . '

'It's dryin' up.'

'But the shock?'

'I resist shocks like a rodeo bull.'

'You are impossible!' she gasped, and he swung his stockinged feet over the side of the bunk and sat for a few moments until his senses stopped reeling.

'You can get me my boots,' he said

finally. 'Kinda strange how you always seem to see me with my boots off!'

'Where do you think you're going?'

'To Delta!' he said with all the terrible finality of a man who cannot escape some damnable sense of urgent fate. 'To see three men . . . and that's where they'll be . . . '

'But — they'll kill you — Jim Gallery!'

'No — I'll kill them . . . '

She stared at him fearfully, her warm brown eyes pools of horror. He looked at her sideways, quizzically, the Irish heritage now deep in his facial outlines. The raw wound gave him a lopsided appearance and emphasised his grim, earnest mood. He wasn't fooling.

'Why? Why kill them? Why not just let them disappear?'

'They'll get around to learning that I'm not dead — some day, and come ridin' and gunnin' for me again. Those three men want me dead, Helen. They have a burr in their minds about me — just like it is with me. They just won't rest if they know I'm alive. You see, they hate me. D'you know the kind of hate they've got, Helen?'

'I don't even want to know . . . '

'I guess not, but I'll tell you. They hate me for many reasons and they'll thrust through any damned danger or hardship to see me lyin' like a corpse — because that's the only kind of answer that'll give them any satisfaction. They want the finality of a lifeless body! They see brutality and death as a kind of religion. It's the only medicine they know and they aim to hand it to me. They'll do just that — if they figure I recovered. They'll come right back lookin' for me — to corpse!'

'And you want to hand them the same treatment?' she searched his face for truths.

'I guess so — but not because of hate!' He took her hand. 'Believe this, Helen. It isn't hate. It's survival. They hate — I survive.'

She moved away restlessly. She stood at the window and looked out at the night. 'You won't be put off, I see. I'll go and get the horses ready . . . '

'Horses?'

'I'm going with you. I have friends in Delta. And someone should notify the deputy sheriff about Mack Slater — you might be too busy killing,' she said grimly.

Nothing he could say would deter her. If he was obstinate, she intended to show him that she, too, could have the same streak. But there were other reasons; he might fall from his horse through a sudden weakness and she wanted to be there.

He got ready slowly, drawing on reserves of deep, inner energy. He had to force himself through most of the preparations, but he would not admit this to the girl. Finally, he was all set, his boots on, a Colt .45 in a holster, spare slugs in the pocket of his flapping vest and a hat on his head. He had borrowed the hat; his other one was lying out somewhere in the rocks. He went out to the tierail, where the girl had left the horses after rounding them up down in the grassy, sandy hollows among the rocky sentinels.

'It'll be a slow ride to Delta,' she warned. 'It's dark — and you can't ride at full lope . . . '

'You're nurse-maidin' me again!' he grinned. 'But I'm telling you something, Helen — when we hit Delta you get goin' to your friends and I'll mosey around.'

There was no way to defy him or argue the point. Bert Mackay stood at the tierail to see them off. Helen had a rifle in the saddle-scabbard — and for that matter she had seen to it that Jim Gallery's mount was similarly equipped. For a girl who didn't like killing, she knew the value of guns for a cause that was right.

They cantered easily away from the Yellow Stones area and took to the faintly discernible trail that led to Delta. Thankfully, a glimpse of moon helped them, while she watched Jim Gallery closely as he sat hard in the saddle. He did not sway or show signs of faintness. He hunched grimly and, as the miles sped under rapidly moving hoofs, he said little.

She tried to speak to him. 'What are your plans?'

'Just look . . . '

'You mean in saloons?'

'Yep. Where else in a town like Delta, and with owlhoots like them three . . . '

'You — you — just intend to start a fight?'

'Maybe.'

'You're not very talkative, Jim!'

'I got a sore head, Miss Mackay — and lousy thoughts.'

'We could go back — forget about those men.'

He almost snarled, 'You know that's impossible!'

She was silent after that, not wanting to annoy him. He'd had a grim time — and he had a conscience; she would not contribute to his tribulations. But if only he'd turn back!

They rode into town and the girl

pointed to the light gleaming inside the sheriff's office.

'The deputy is still there. Won't you go and see him?'

'You do it, Helen. You know who killed him — two hellions by the name of Stephen Crane and Max Kerle. The latter is wanted right throughout Wyoming.'

She handed him a taut, wary smile and left him. She couldn't change his mind, his grim intent.

He didn't barge right into the first saloon. Even with his savage need to rid himself of these men, he knew it was an encounter which needed to be approached slowly and with due respect.

He wished he had the makings for a cigarette. The habit wasn't one he indulged in very often but, right now, he thought he needed the consoling weed. With the girl vanished into the night, he felt suddenly and unpleasantly alone — in the full stark sense of the word!

Yeah, if he didn't kill them, they'd hunt him again when they heard he was alive. That was the measure of their hate . . . But now, because of their ignorance of events, he had the advantage . . .

He knew Delta like the back of his hand; all the streets, banks, stores, livery stables, saloons. He knew the saloons particularly, for he was that kind of man, and a saloon was a place for men tired of sweaty horses and warm saddles. He walked stiffly towards the first one. The sound of a tinny piano impinged on his ears as he walked.

Jim Gallery stood at the batwings and glanced warily into the interior. The noise was pretty deafening, with some man singing a mournful ditty created by some sad gent during the Civil War. He stared swiftly at the tables; saw a collection of gamblers dressed in assorted garments from buckskin to top hats, smoking cigars and having a rare night out.

He eased warily away; there was no sign here of the three killers. He went to his horse, led it away down the street to where light spilled in flickering yellow beams from another saloon. He was hitching the leathers around a tierail when he became aware of two horses at the end of the main stem. He glanced tiredly, a mere flick of his eyes. The horses were a good three hundred yards away, moving away from him and heading out of town, and only one horse had a rider. The other was being led.

After the first narrowed glance Jim Gallery stiffened, hand flashing to his gun — and then he just became hesitant.

He thought he'd seen Stephen Crane riding a big black but the night air seemed a bit hazy at that end of the main stem. Surely he was suffering delusions . . . and why the horse with the empty saddle . . . was it not just some horseman of the same build?

Jim Gallery wiped sweaty hands

147

down the sides of his pants. He thought he should stick to his original idea that the three men would be found together in a saloon. That had to be their destination. They just wouldn't have any other business at that time of night. They'd be relaxing, thinking they'd left him for dead.

He took three big strides to the batwings of the saloon, stared grimly into the smoke-haze, and like the crack of a gun two figures impacted vividly on to his brain.

Max Kerle and Kid Dawson were there, standing with their backs to him, hunched, with elbows solid on the bar and making out with talk and loud laughs. Two men . . . the ones he sought but where was Crane?

And then he knew that he had in fact seen Stephen Crane slowly riding down the street, disappearing into the gloom at the end of the stem. His first thought had been right. Tiredness, the wound in his head, something had affected his judgment momentarily. It was now too late to tackle the man. He had two right before him . . .

For some moments Jim Gallery waited, sombre, a certain tinge of grim distaste in his gut. He began to detest the gunhawks. They were living, moving proof that all men had the killer streak in them. They were dragging him down to that level. Sure, he wanted them dead — but he wished someone else would do the killing. And he was heavy with the knowledge that his first conviction was right; they'd return to hunt him the day they knew he was not dead.

Still he waited, moving to one side as a big man pushed through the batwings and handed him a surly stare.

Where was Stephen Crane going? He certainly wasn't taking the animals to some livery because he was heading for the black fringes on the rim of the town. Had this lot finally argued and fallen out?

He threw another glance at Max Kerle and Kid Dawson as they shifted stance at the bar and laughed loudly. These two were pretty pally for a change. What was the good humour in aid of? Just drink?

Finally, almost reluctantly, thinking oddly enough of Helen Mackay, he edged into the saloon and found a space between two tables. There were no men between him and the other two rannigans.

'Kerle! Dawson!' He shouted above the din. Then again. 'Kerle! Dawson! Turn around — I want you two!'

Something in the deadly tones bit into the brains of the other two men and they turned — and then froze. Jim Gallery was a ghost — with a hand hovering above a gun, his body in the gunfighter's stance!

9

One Man Less

'You — Gallery — you should be dead!' It was Max Kerle's gasping statement.

Kid Dawson added his angry comment, 'That Crane — the galoot's a liar! Always foolin' me . . . '

'He looked plumb dead,' said Max Kerle. 'I was there, Kid.'

'You two rats gunned down the sheriff,' Jim Gallery grated. 'But that ain't rilin' me just now. You know I want to kill you two . . . '

'Figure to take us together, Gallery!' jeered Max Kerle. His brain was working swiftly, unaffected by the drink now that danger sharpened his senses. He thought that two guns could beat one — even if one man stopped a slug. It wouldn't be Maxy boy, because he knew a trick or two, he sure did . . . but the Kid might stop a bullet.

'I'll take you — or die . . . ' Jim Gallery watched them tautly, nerves tingling into ultra awareness. Everything else fled his mind. He saw only two men in a sharply delineated sense of the present. Nothing else mattered — except the signs that gave them away. He noted the way Kid Dawson twitched; the slow hunch that indicated Max Kerle was going to act.

Men in the saloon inched away. The card tables became round surfaces where cards ceased to move, and the players sat stiffly. But one man had seized on a significant fact.

'Killed the sheriff!' he echoed. 'Now who the hell says that?'

'I say it,' snapped Jim Gallery, his eyes fixed on the two men.

'Mack Slater — dead! Why, he was a great feller! Them murderin' skunks done it, you say?'

'I say it.'

The man muttered angrily, turned to others. 'Mack Slater's dead! Now ain't

152

that real bad! He was a real good *hombre* . . . '

'Real good *hombres* die just the same as other men,' said Jim Gallery grimly. 'And these two hellions helped kill him — along with another gunny.'

'Crane!' muttered Kid Dawson. 'Where in hell is Crane?'

'Lightin' out, I think,' said Jim Gallery. 'I just seen him leading another horse . . . saddled . . . '

'The gold!' cursed Max Kerle. 'Hell, that bastard has the gold — I bet! Sure! What else? Gawd, I've been fooled!'

'What damned gold are you yappin' about, Kerle?' Jim Gallery asked.

'The gold we lifted from two galoots way back on the trail,' sneered the other. 'Yeah, we struck it rich, Gallery — and I'm gonna live to spend it . . . '

'Gold?' The lean man's eyes narrowed. 'You mean four sacks?'

'We do — if it's any business of yours, Gallery . . . '

'The girl and her pa at Yellow Stones had gold stolen from them . . . '

'Sure — and we lifted it from the two jiggers that rode out with it. And we got horses — after you left us to walk . . . '

'And now Stephen Crane has ridden out with the lot!' mocked Jim Gallery. 'Ain't that somethin'!'

Max Kerle could stand the situation no longer. He clawed for his gun in a frenzy of fury, not only at Jim Gallery but at being tricked by Stephen Crane, the smooth rogue with the English accent. He had a blazing vision of the man riding away, laughing, carrying the gold that meant so much.

Max Kerle was angry, but that did not affect his judgment and the plan he knew he had to put over.

Kid Dawson dived for his gun. His two hands rammed down together, but one went to an invisible holster. He wished — cursingly — that he had his twin guns, the ones he'd been so fast with.

As Max Kerle hauled his sixgun from leather, he dived with astonishing speed to his right, firing swiftly. Two shots spat out. Kid Dawson triggered wildly as his Colt whipped up — and then he staggered forward blindly as a hole appeared in his forehead and his life force was shattered.

The shots from Max Kerle's gun hissed over Jim Gallery's head, proving that a man can be too hasty. The hawk-like man had intended to blast Jim Gallery between the eyes, but in diving, his gun had angled slightly.

Jim Gallery felt the slugs cut air above his head and he flinched. Kid Dawson's solitary shot was affected by the way his body jerked under the impact of Jim Gallery's slug and the bullet flew to the saloon ceiling. Then the Kid crumpled.

In diving to the right, Max Kerle avoided the shot that Jim Gallery blasted at him by a fraction of an inch — and then the cunning range rider rammed into a table, upsetting it. The heavy lump of pine thudded on to its side, providing a shield for Max Kerle.

Jim Gallery hunched, triggered off

another shot. This bit deep into the table and stayed there. Max Kerle whipped off a chance shot, poking out his head and hand momentarily. Jim fired at him, but again the man dodged death by a split-second. And Max Kerle's fast shot was obviously wide — but it scattered men in the saloon like frightened chickens in a farmyard.

Max Kerle knew he had to keep moving — or die. He reached out, grabbed a chair leg and hurled the thing right over the table and into Jim Gallery. As Jim staggered, ducking involuntarily, Max Kerle rushed to the door at the side of the saloon. Right there, in his mind, with implacable fury, was only one thought; to get away and hunt Stephen Crane. Sudden blazing hatred of the man overcame even his dislike of Jim Gallery.

The chair halted Jim Gallery sufficiently to allow Max Kerle to grab at the door handle and wrench the thing open. As he darted into the black night, another shot from Jim's gun blasted after him and chipped wood splinters from the wall where Kerle's head had been only a second previously.

And then Max Kerle was escaping into the night, darting behind a building, moving like a mountain cat in his rage. When Jim Gallery stared out of the doorway, the man had gone. He was about to follow Max Kerle when a man touched his arm. Jim Gallery turned swiftly, still jaggedly alert. He saw a solid-looking man who obviously had something to say.

'Them gents rode into town with a pack of horse-flesh. Fifty head. They got them in the old corral . . . '

'Fifty horses?' Jim growled. 'Where'n hell did they get them?'

'I dunno . . . they told the corral owner they figured to sell 'em tomorrow.'

'Did you see the three men in here?'

'Sure thing. One went out — not so long ago — the tall galoot with the greyin' hair . . . '

'Stephen Crane . . . I saw him . . . '

Jim Gallery was talking to himself.

'Them gents booked in at the Star Hotel — I was told by the corral owner — '

The Star Hotel! Jim Gallery knew the place. The hunch hit him that Max Kerle would have his horse stabled for the night not too far from the same hotel. And Kerle would need a horse.

Jim Gallery rushed out of the saloon. If the deputy was around he could sort out the facts behind Kid Dawson's death, and maybe Helen Mackay could help in that direction.

He leaped into the saddle of his horse but before he could rowel the animal forward a man strode out of the saloon and grabbed the headstall. 'Hey, you said the sheriff was dead! Mack Slater dead?'

'That's right. They killed him. Let go that harness, mister . . . '

'Now look, I was a pal of Mack Slater. How come he got killed?'

'He was just gunned down. Quit hangin' on to that leather, pardner, I want to go . . . '

'That corpse in there one of the killers?'

'He was one of the three . . . '

Jim Gallery nudged his horse and the man had to stop detaining him. But time had been wasted. He set the animal into a full lope down the street and hauled it up before the cheap hotel. Then he decided Max Kerle could be at the livery.

It was obvious that Kerle knew where Stephen Crane was going. The man had the gold — the sacks that had been stolen from Helen Mackay and her father. So they had intercepted the two robbers who had originally lifted the valuable bags of nuggets. It wasn't difficult to guess at the fate of those two men. They would be dead, just targets for slugs. And they had taken horses from the men. It all added up, but where did the fifty horses fit in?

'Who the devil did they rob to get them?' Jim mused grimly.

That problem hardly mattered for the moment. So Stephen Crane had lit out with the stolen gold, finally double-crossing his two partners! Well, that figured! It was in character! Gold had distorted the minds of better men than Stephen Crane . . .

With all the tension of the past events crowding him, Jim Gallery felt a throbbing in his head. The wound felt raw, almost protesting.

He had to get going. Where was Max Kerle? At the livery — or in the hotel grabbing at his gear?

Jim finally figured that the man would be at the livery when all at once the rapid thud of hoofs indicated a rider thrusting a horse to full gallop. A dark shape, crouching low on a horse, raced around the block and tore into the night.

Jim Gallery nudged his animal into instant chase and he hauled out his handgun. He pumped off two shots at the distant, shadowy target and then realized his gun was empty when it clicked stupidly. He thrust it back to leather.

But it soon became obvious that Max Kerle was not riding the mount that had taken him into Delta, for the horse was strong and fresh and its pounding hoofs took the man swiftly along the out-going trail. A stand of cottonwoods loomed up like black shadows in the night and Jim Gallery could barely see the rider and horse ahead. Kerle had grabbed at some saddled mount in the livery, a good horse. In that gunslinger's catalogue of crimes horse stealing was the least heinous.

He seemed to have some destination in mind. Jim's hunch became stronger; Max Kerle knew where to find Stephen Crane — and the tantalising gold!

That glittering metal, so hardly won, belonged to Helen Mackay and her father! So he'd be damned if he'd let these rats take it! In any case there would surely be a rumpus if and when Max Kerle caught up with Stephen Crane. Someone might end up dead.

Jim Gallery muttered grimly, peering ahead, seeing only odd glimpses of the swiftly moving rider whose horse was pounding along the trail. His own animal was tired and not in the same class as the mount that Kerle had grabbed. Would the man lose him?

For a moment he considered taking a chance number of shots at Max Kerle, using the rifle in the saddle scabbard, but it was very dicey because the man was drawing well ahead. And then he knew he wanted to let Max Kerle locate Stephen Crane, not because he might annihilate him, but because this might lead to the recovery of the gold that belonged to Helen and her father. It was important.

So for the time being it was a chase and an uncertain one at that. The other man was well ahead, somewhere on the black trail, and Jim's horse was blowing. The unequal contest could not last much longer because Max Kerle would draw so far ahead he would be lost.

Grimly, tiredly, his head throbbing again, he felt his old mixture of hatred and disgust for these men. One was dead. Was it two to go? The gold belonged to Helen — and this was a new intent in his life; he'd see that she and her father retrieved the gold they had worked so hard for.

And then what? Would he seek out Harry Carslake and the missing loot from the Drago Cattlemen's Bank? Or was he becoming sick and tired of it all?

He hardly knew what prompted these thoughts but there was this mental vision of Helen and the disapproval there would be in her brown eyes if he told her all the truth about himself. He'd been lawless. He'd been a gunhand but he had only killed when challenged, and in self-defence. Somewhere, deep inside him, he felt that the lawless life was fading out as a way of living for him — and he knew Helen had made him feel that way.

These thoughts, momentary, fleeting, taking little time to flash through a tired mind, dispersed again when he thought he saw a dark shape of rider and horse leave the trail and, with long leaps, climb the steeply rising ground to the right. It was Max Kerle, he was sure, moving off the trail. A stand of old oaks blurred into a mass of darkness and swallowed the other rider. Where was he going?

Well, he just had to follow, trusting to luck. He had a feeling they were only about two miles out of town, but it had been a fast ride. The horse was tuckered out, nostrils flaring, eyes gleaming wildly.

He got another glimpse of the rider ahead when his horse breasted a rise and he was momentarily a dark shape against a slightly lighter shade of gloom, and then he was gone, but the sighting was enough for Jim Gallery. He urged his animal into another snorting gallop.

★　★　★

Max Kerle pressed on towards the old, ruined adobe walls of the mission just ahead, and there was the shack — a light glinting thinly from the one window.

Crane was there! He'd gotten a good start — and he was there with the gold and the darned girl on whom he had fixed his lecherous eyes. Of all this there was no doubt. Whether Crane knew he would be followed was a matter for conjecture; the hardcase must have known there was the possibility that he'd be followed.

Max Kerle cursed the pursuer behind him. Without the nuisance of Jim Gallery he could have dealt with Stephen Crane in his own good time. There was only one thing to do with a skunk; back-shooting was too good for him! A knife in the ribs was one way to deal with the sarcastic swine who had needled him for so long. The knife was great for revenge; a man could stab repeatedly, savouring the full flavour of retribution.

He had a knife. But maybe he would have to use the gun. He would see.

But Jim Gallery was a troublesome, tricky factor in this setup. Could he deal with him first and then Crane?

Max Kerle raced his animal past the gloomy walls of the old mission and then drew the mount up in a swirl of hoof dust. What better place to ambush the following man! Sure, he would kill Jim Gallery first and then tackle Stephen Crane and secure the gold.

Once again he thought about the marvellous silence of the knife. If he could get Jim Gallery with the blade, Crane would not have any cause for alarm. If Crane wasn't warned by some shooting, he could creep up on the rat! And that would be the final killing . . .

On drawing his horse to a halt, Max Kerle wheeled the animal around and nudged it into the shelter of the old adobe walls. He leaped down; didn't bother to hitch the animal. There wasn't time.

He raced to the nearest corner and

peered out, listening. He heard the approaching sound of Jim Gallery's animal; hoofs drumming, a snorting from the tired creature. Delighted, he judged the other rider would race up on a line almost abreast of the old adobe wall.

Max Kerle drew his Bowie knife from the sheath that had been sewn into his gunbelt long ago. It had been a long time since he had used the knife.

But there was no time for reflections no matter how fleeting. The rider was fast approaching . . .

As Jim Gallery's mount stretched protesting legs in the last few yards to the shack where the light proved there was someone inside, Max Kerle leaped out at rider and horse.

The animal whinnied in sudden fear and jerked. The black shape hurtling with all the ferocity of a striking mountain cat scared the horse — and warned Jim Gallery, with only a splintered second in which to react.

And then Max Kerle's arms were

around his waist and he was tugged from the saddle and the horse cantered in fright into the night. As Jim Gallery thudded to earth he saw the sudden gleam in the scant light of the night — and he rolled desperately. bringing the other man over with him.

The Bowie stabbed into the earth, and Jim Gallery knew what he was up against. He recalled Max Kerle's affection for the Bowie knife. But the man evidently had other good reasons for using the knife — silence. And his own Colt was at the moment useless.

The chamber was empty!

10

Enter a Little Man

Stephen Crane reached the shack beside the old ruined mission and dismounted, tying the two horses to the remains of an ancient tierail.

He had the key to the battered but thick old door. It was a key fashioned by some blacksmith and was about seven inches long. He had found it inside the shack when he had left, and so he had tried the lock and found it turned.

He hoped Max Kerle and Kid Dawson were bent upon getting really drunk; that would surely keep them occupied. He opened the door and walked into the cabin. He did not bother to lock the door this time, but stared in admiration and amusement at the bound figure of the fair-haired girl.

He had left the lamp burning low — because he was, after all, a gentleman — and she had apparently been struggling with her bonds. Her face was flushed; her eyes furious. Two buttons on the checked shirt had split away with her struggles and her womanly shape was something his lecherous eyes noted at once.

'Well, my dear, I'm back — to give you some comfort! You didn't imagine I'd leave you here forever, did you?' His mocking tones were as false as his pretences.

'Go away — killer!'

He stood over her; eyed her so deliberately, his gaze travelling over her body with such evil intent, that she paled in fear. Her head flinched back as if to get away from him, but the ropes held her.

'You and I are going to take a little journey.' He placed a tentative hand on her shoulder; gripped hard when he felt the soft flesh underneath the shirt. There was something ominous in his very touch.

She gave a little sob. 'I hate you . . . I hope you die . . . someone will kill you . . . a beast like you . . . a mangey polecat!'

Even the callous nature of this man disliked the pure hate which poured from her. He tried to smile. 'You'll soon get used to me, my dear. You're a woman — although devastatingly youthful — and I have a way with women. You will not hate me for long. You see, we shall travel together . . . share everything . . . and it is the nature of women to submit . . . I know you will accept me — and you might as well start now!'

He began to untie the ropes that bound her to the rickety old chair, but he did not undo the bindings on her wrists. As he worked, his cold eyes stared broodingly at the soft contours of her breasts, so much so that she shuddered.

He attempted an almost ridiculous effort at gallantry. 'You know, I was an officer in a fine regiment — drank only the best wines in India — was attended by native servants — had my own batman. I was in a splendid position until — until — well, that hardly matters now. I mention this, my dear girl, to show you that you have nothing to fear — if you only do as I say!'

Her reply was swift and earthy. 'You're a swine! A rogue — like my pa would say!' And now that she was free to struggle, she hit out at him with her fists bound together.

The retaliation enraged Stephen Crane and knocked a hole in his attempt at dignity. Her lithe young fists hammered into his face; she twisted like a cat turning on some canine attacker. He gave a snarl of anger that swept away his pretence and then he had to hit her. It was a hard blow that would have hurt any man. She sank dazedly to the ground, her corn-coloured head lowered.

'Damn you! Of all the she-cats! I think a thrashing with a belt is the medicine to teach you humility — and give me some pleasure!'

He unbuckled the two-inch wide leather belt which encircled him and flailed it. His gunbelt sagged around him.

'You asked for it, my dear.' His features were twisted in an expression befitting any sadist. 'A little lesson — and then we shall have to hit the trail because there are gun-happy men who must know where to find me . . .

★ ★ ★

The little man crouched in half-witted fear in a corner made by two crumbling walls of the old mission and he watched the ferocious fight that ensued between the two men in a sort of scared fascination. His steeple-shaped hat, ragged, full of holes, was pulled down almost to his eyebrows and his blanket was wrapped tightly around him, for Mungo Casson knew how to huddle in a corner for the night. He had been living inside the old walls for some weeks, without benefit of a roof, and making a weekly trip to Delta — on foot because he owned nothing — to scrounge for anything that was useful to a bum who had no intelligence or inclination for work.

The fight on the open ground just outside the walls scared him to hell. But he watched, like some creature of the night witnessing a struggle between giants. And Mungo was afraid.

Men who fought might turn on him — if he revealed himself. And how they fought! Two men rolling over and over on the earth. The sounds of their scuffle came harshly to his ears. They rammed fists at each other — and something gleamed for a moment. A knife! These men would kill! He, Mungo Casson, would let them kill each other while he hugged his comforting corner.

And for Jim Gallery it really seemed like a fight to the death. For one thing the wound on his head began to throb again. And Max Kerle seemed possessed by all the fury of the devil. No doubt the rannigan was crazed with anger against Stephen Crane. The man had the gold.

Jim Gallery had seen the light in the shack; guessed that Crane had made for this place. Why, he wasn't sure. Did the man think it a hideout for the night? And Max Kerle had known exactly where to find Crane. Strange . . . but right now he had a fight for survival on his hands.

He held the man's knife at bay, using all his strength, grimacing with the effort. The throb in his head seemed to warn him that his strength was not unlimited. Kerle glared down at him, his face a mask in the faint light. He jerked sideways, loosening Jim Gallery's grip on his knife hand. Kerle slashed down again — and Jim rolled, but only a few inches because Kerle was on top of him and his weight was pinning him down.

The knife sliced past Jim's ear and made a cut in the ground. Kerle jerked it free again and as it moved Jim Gallery punched at the man's face. His fist connected, a desperate blow that had all his energy behind it. Max Kerle gasped like a hog kicked in the belly. But the knife was still in his grip. A man could stand a number of blows but a knife wound could put paid to his chances. Jim Gallery knew he just had to get that knife out of the man's fist . . .

Jim Gallery brought up a boot and kicked at the other man, ramming it into his crotch. It was a vicious blow and caught Kerle unawares. The man was concentrating all his efforts on using his knife. The pain from the boot made him howl and momentarily pause in the fight. Jim Gallery thrust the man back with two bunched fists and then scrambled to his feet. He felt better on his feet.

He came at Max Kerle again, determined to end the fight. He'd use any means in his power. If his gun had been loaded, he'd have shot the man where he lay. But it was empty and there wasn't time for loading. But he could use it as a club.

Swinging the weapon, the butt-end hacking through the air, he came at Max Kerle as the man scrambled to his feet. Jim lunged with the gunbutt and missed; Kerle had leaped back. Then the other man came in, his knife upraised, the ugly look on his face indicating that he wanted to kill and finish with this fight.

As the knife thrust at his throat, Jim Gallery swayed back and missed the vicious blade by the thickness of a playing card.

Then, quick as a flash, with hellish strength surging through him, his gunbutt hacked down. It connected with Max Kerle's cranium and the man sank. Even as his knees buckled, Jim Gallery rushed in again and grabbed at the almost limp knife hand. He twisted the blade from the man's hand and flung it far into the night. At that moment Max Kerle sagged to the ground, unconscious for the moment.

Jim looked down savagely. After a pause of about two seconds, during which he dragged in fresh night air to gasping lungs, he began to load his Colt.

The gun ready, he pointed it at the unconscious man. And then he hesitated. For a crazy moment he wondered who he was to mete out this kind of justice. And he saw Helen Mackay's face somewhere in the darkness. Another crazy delusion, but it was enough to deter him. His gun lowered.

He knew that Kerle was wanted for murder in Wyoming — and possibly elsewhere. And he had been a party to the killing of the sheriff. The law could hang him.

Jim Gallery sucked in air and almost groaned. He knew right then that he was sick and tired of the law of the gun; that he had little right to kill even a rat like Kerle in cold blood. Maybe self-defence, but that was all. He holstered his gun.

There was still Stephen Crane and the gold. If the man was inside that shack, the gold would be with him. He had no right to it.

Jim Gallery bent over the unconscious Max Kerle and took off the man's bandanna and then, rolling him over, he tied his hands behind his back with the neckerchief. Then Jim took his own bandanna and used it to bind Kerle's ankles together. That would immobilise the ruffian until he could be handed over to the law and a fair trial.

Jim Gallery straightened; looked at the shack which lay not so far away.

Jim carried Max Kerle into a corner of the old walled mission courtyard and dumped him. The man could be retrieved later. Even as he dropped the heavy body, he heard the man groan. So he was coming round! Well, he wouldn't escape those bonds in a hurry!

Jim Gallery went to look for his horse. He found two animals; there was Kerle's mount, nibbling at some tufts of grass, and his own horse wasn't too far away.

He held his own horse by the reins and decided to stick with it. The other animal had an owner somewhere. The horse he held had originally belonged to Kid Dawson — not that he would be objecting!

Jim Gallery walked slowly and grimly towards the shack. He knew he had to concentrate his wits on this new problem. Why, for instance, was Stephen Crane in this place?

Even as Jim Gallery disappeared into the night, moving to the shack and the problem of Stephen Crane and the gold, a little man crawled out of a corner of the mission walls like some rodent seeking a scrap of food.

Little Mungo, with his wits addled by years of sun and lonely living, was curious, now that the fight had ceased. He could see pretty well in the dark, strangely enough, and he knew there was a bundle in the corner of the courtyard. It was a man. He looked dead. The other big man had left him for dead. There were always pickings on the dead . . .

Mungo Casson pulled his thin blanket tightly around him and scuttled over, warily, for he was a timid man. He crouched over the bound body and blinked. Then the man gave a groan — and Mungo nearly ran away!

But, unusually brave, he stayed and listened. The man made rasping, dirty noises in his throat, opened his eyes and glared at the strange shape before him.

'You — who the hell are you?'

'Mungo — just Mungo . . . ' The little bum got ready to run. Then he added with some peculiar pride, 'I kinda live here.'

Max Kerle struggled up, realized he was bound at the same time that recollections of the fight between him and Jim Gallery flooded back. So the coyote had beaten him! Bound him — the hell!

Kerle stared at the little hunched shape in the blanket. 'Hey — you —

untie these blamed kerchiefs.'

'I — I — can't. You'll hit me . . . Mungo don't like bein' hit . . . '

Max Kerle suppressed an urge to curse the odd little man. 'Get me outa this,' he breathed. 'I'll give you money . . . '

'Dollars?'

'Anything you want . . . just get me free . . . '

'I dunno . . . Mungo scared . . . '

'Look, I got money. Now just untie these kerchiefs! You can do it! I won't hurt you — that's a promise, pardner . . . '

But the odd little man, with fear of everything moving, took a lot of convincing. Valuable time passed . . .

11

The Fatal Gunplay

Jim Gallery slowly approached the rough old shack, leading his horse, his eyes fixed grimly on the low yellow light behind the solitary window. As he came up, he saw the two horses hitched outside the place. One was the smaller saddled animal he was sure he had seen Stephen Crane leading away at the darkened end of the main street in Delta. Now why did the man want a second horse?

The need for caution was so obvious that Jim Gallery halted and left his horse standing. The animal just stood, tired, head drooping. It sure wouldn't go far if he needed it! He checked his gun. Loaded! Ready to kill again? He compressed his lips, fatigue tugging at his guts, and knew he would use the gun in self-defence only. The old premise of hunting Kerle and Stephen Crane because they would hunt him seemed to have ebbed from him. He wished he could explain to Helen Mackay, but she was in Delta and she still thought he was seeking vengeance.

He was, in a sense. He intended to see that the gold went to the rightful owners. They had worked hard for it . . .

He stood in the night air, his wits sharpened to the oddities of this situation because there was something strange about Stephen Crane's presence in this rough shack. Why did he want two horses?

That the man had the gold there was no doubt, but why he should make for this shack seemed a mystery. Kerle had known exactly where to find him. Surely if Crane had wanted to lose himself in the night he would not have gone to a place where he knew the other men would locate him? So he had a reason for visiting this shack! Could be some small detail — guns — grub — maps . . .

While Jim Gallery was musing grimly on the probabilities, his gun in his hand, a scream tore out of the old shack like the cry of someone in agony! Surprised, shocked, Jim Gallery realized the sound came from a woman's throat. A woman in there with Crane?

There was inevitably a moment when he froze and thought swiftly over the facts. What the hell had Crane gotten into? A woman! He had heard tales before about Stephen Crane's strange taste in women . . . Was this the reason why Crane had travelled to this shack and not hightailed it for the open range?

He walked forward after the momentary pause. His Colt poked out like a grim symbol of justice. He'd use it — swiftly — if need be in spite of his doubts and uncertainties . . .

He reached the shack door and noticed that it was slightly ajar. At that moment another frightened scream vibrated from inside the cabin and a girl's voice was heard.

'Don't! Please . . . don't . . . ah . . . '

There was a sound like a whip — or leather — slapping hard against something — and the girl's cry came again. Then he heard Crane's snarled advice. 'Shut up! You young idiot — I'm merely teaching you a lesson. There's no need to wake the dead! Some women actually like this sort of thing!'

Jim Gallery rammed the door flat back as if he would crash it off the hinges. At the same time, in one swift motion, his legs took him into the cabin. One glance was enough!

'Drop that belt, Crane — or by God I'll puncture your gut!' The big man turned in surprise, the belt hanging limply, his cold eyes glinting when he saw Jim Gallery.

'You! My God — you should be dead!'

The girl widened her eyes and ran to a corner of the shack. Her hands were bound, Jim Gallery noted grimly, but her feet were free. She shouted, 'Help me — please — help me!'

'Drop that belt, Crane,' Jim snarled. 'You damned swine — so it's true what they say about you and women . . . ?'

Jim's Colt poked forward like some grimly metallic machine ready for bloodied reprisal, and Stephen Crane swayed in doubt. His first significant act was to drop the belt, and then he returned to his astonished realization that Jim Gallery was indeed alive.

'You were dead — I was sure of it — how the hell did you get here?'

'You answer some questions, *amigo*,' rapped Jim. 'Who is this girl? I won't ask you what you're doin' with her . . .'

'She's just some young bitch — '

'I'm Delia Breen!' cried the girl. 'Help me! My father was the mustanger — they stole our horses — killed my poor pa!'

'Ah, the fifty horses!' Jim nodded. 'I wondered how they fitted . . .'

'We were on the trail to Delta and these dirty skunks rode down on us and just shot my pa in cold blood . . . '

'That figures,' Jim said tightly.

'They made me go with them . . . tied . . . to those Yellow Stones . . . and then after some fight in the hills they came back . . . drove the horses to Delta . . . '

'You don't need to tell me any more.' Jim Gallery swung to Stephen Crane. 'Seein' we're doin' a lot of talkin', you might as well know that Kid Dawson is dead and Kerle came gunnin' for you . . . '

'Where the devil is he?'

'Outside — in the dark — tied like a hog. I'm handing him over to the law . . . '

Stephen Crane laughed and relaxed. His body eased from the tense attitude he'd taken; his right hand hovered just above his gunbutt. It was something that Jim Gallery noted without expression.

'You know, Gallery, you and I could do a neat little deal — unless you want to court death . . . '

'Go on,' said the other man.

'Gold is a fascinating material, don't you agree? Men fight and die for it — not that we have to do that! We can share this valuable metal . . . ride out . . . as partners . . . '

'All right . . . '

'You agree?' Stephen Crane was surprised — and suspicious.

'Yeah — just drop your gunbelt — slowly . . . '

The big man with the cunning mind saw the trick coming up. 'That isn't a deal, Gallery. You just want to disarm me.'

'It was worth a try . . . '

Stephen Crane's hand twitched fractionally closer to the gun lying snugly in the shiny holster. 'You'll have to do better than that, Gallery. Let's talk it over — as gentlemen — '

'I'm no gent,' snapped Jim, 'and you're something that crawled out of hog's dung!'

'Put that gun in leather and insult me again!' The other man's fury was slowly rising. His face had paled. 'Just give me a chance . . . '

'You never gave any man a fightin' chance in your life,' snapped Jim Gallery, 'but — all right — you can go for your iron when you like.'

And the lean, tired man with the wary scowl on his Irish face shoved his gun into the holster. Crane could draw when he liked! But Stephen Crane paused, his brain racing, scheming.

'Gold, Gallery, you idiot! Don't you realize it's a fair amount of money — shared just two ways! Damn, you bucked the law for less than that! Are you trying to adopt a halo in your latter days? What's wrong with you, Gallery? Don't you like money?'

'It's all there — outside — ain't it?' said Jim with a queer smile. 'I could start shootin' and kill you and then ride off with the gold!'

'I might kill you!'

'You might!' Jim nodded.

'Look, I'll let the girl go free!' Stephen Crane licked dry lips. 'She's nothing to me — just a diversion.'

'You've been givin' her hell, you ageing swine . . .'

'She can go! Damn it! All I want is the gold.'

'When you're ready, Crane.' Jim Gallery's eyes glinted in the faint yellow light. The girl stared in fascination, speechless for the moment, sensing the hate and remorseless inner pressures of these two men. 'Go for that iron just any time you like.'

A silence fell that seemed to last for a horrifying time, and then with a speed that was starkly paralysing to the girl the two men clawed for guns.

Crack! Crack!

The two shots exploded inside the shack like cannons from a barricade. Both men had hunched. Both men held smoking guns.

Stephen Crane smiled for a long time. Jim Gallery watched him, frozen in his last attitude.

Stephen Crane smiled as his gun sank. Redness had time to soak into his shirt as his heart pumped on in the last few seconds of life, and then he fell slowly sideways — and forwards — and hit the wood planks of the cabin floor.

The girl shrieked again and again. Jim Gallery holstered his gun and strode over to her. He placed a comforting arm around her shoulders. 'You'll be all right, gal. Don't be too afraid. He had it coming . . . '

'Please get me out of here! Oh, I wish I could see my pa . . . '

'You'll get to Delta,' said Jim. 'There's a horse outside. Go to the sheriff's office and ask for the deputy. Then ask for a woman called Helen Mackay. Tell her everythin' . . . '

'I don't want to ride alone . . . '

'Waal, it's only two miles.'

'I — I — want you to go with me.'

Jim Gallery grinned crookedly. 'You trust me — after this galoot?'

'I can trust you — I know! I'll ride back with you to Delta.'

'All right,' said the lean, tired man. 'Fine. But I've got some little chores, gal. This body will have to be tied over a hoss. And then there's a hellion outside who'll need fixin' to another horse. All little chores, but we'll get them done — and then ride for town. Maybe this is the end of the line, it is for this so-called gentleman — Stephen Crane! I can't damn his soul because he never had one. And there's another outside . . . '

*   *   *

But right at that moment Max Kerle was free. The odd little man, Mungo Casson, in his foolishness, had untied the range crook. Kerle had sent him running in terror with a wild blow. The bum had served a purpose.

Eyes glinting with a smouldering rage against Jim Gallery, Kerle knew he still had a chance. He could kill Gallery and enrich himself at the same time. The gold was there. But he was weaponless. Gallery had thrown the knife away and taken his gun, too

— probably disposing of it. But there would be guns for a man who had surprise on his side!

As he stood up, churning over his raging thoughts, wishing he could strangle Gallery with his bare hands, he heard the sharp report of two gunshots. Jerking his head, he knew they came from the cabin.

Who had killed whom?

With his arms hanging limply by his sides, his fists clenched in anger, he lurched forward. His head ached with the blow he had received from Jim Gallery's gunbutt.

Even as he moved on, dirt and sweat caked on his face, he knew the need for caution, but even so he was impelled by sheer hate to go after Gallery. And yet maybe there was a change; maybe Crane had annihilated the lean, rock-hard nuisance. Maybe Gallery was lying dead. He might have to deal with Crane again!

There just wasn't any room for hesitation because he hated both men with the same gutsy desire to see them lying dead. Crane had tried to do him out of the gold. Gallery had figured to hand him over to the law.

Max Kerle crept up to the shack, expectant, wary as a wolf. He saw the two horses at the tierail and noted one thing instantly; the gold sacks were still tied to the saddlehorn of the big animal! And only some yards away was the horse that Jim Gallery had used, standing with a tired droop to its head.

Max Kerle thought swiftly. There was a rifle in the saddle-scabbard of Jim Gallery's horse. Well, he needed that! And there was the gold, all there for the taking! Hell, things couldn't be better! It just proved that a real hardcase should never give up.

And yet the need to know who had survived the shots was so strong that it was like a craving. Was Gallery alive? Maybe Crane was dead!

Max Kerle slowly withdrew the rifle from the saddle holster and quietly checked the action. Pressing his ear close to the thick walls of the shack, he could hear some muffled talk. He imagined one voice was that of the girl — but the other? Was it Gallery or Crane?

Drawing in a deep breath, he felt the old hate for both men rise in his throat like a poison. He wanted them dead. And yet — there was the gold! It was a real fortune now that it would be shared with no others! He could have it — the lot! And yet this dirty, insistent need to kill jagged at his mind, almost tauntingly. He had a gun with which to get a quick bead on the man inside. Was it Gallery or Crane?

Max Kerle waited outside the door, the rifle levelled, a leer on his sweat-grimed visage.

He figured he would wait. The man inside the shack would emerge sooner or later. He'd walk into the night and into a shot from the rifle that would blast him into a pain-wracked heap. It was easy and he could not miss. He just had to wait.

He could not be sure if there was talk or activity going on inside the cabin or not. The walls were thick planking, hand-hacked by some unknown who had thought the spot was ideal for some use.

Max Kerle waited, hate swirling into his throat like bile. He'd blast the man who walked out of that door. Would it be Gallery or Crane?

Then there was a footstep and another — crunching into dirt — and they were right behind him. They just did not come from the doorway.

It seemed impossible and he whirled. For a nightmarish moment he saw the menacing figure; the Irish cut of visage that he hated.

Gallery!

He levelled the rifle that had momentarily sagged. But the gun did not explode. Max Kerle had allowed surprise to get the better of him.

An angry boot kicked out like a hammer from hell. Kerle's rifle was rammed up and backwards. The man had to make a frantic attempt to retain his grip on the weapon and while he was doing that Jim Gallery bundled into him, sheer anger urging him to lay hands on the man rather than resort to a handgun.

It was a mistake but he wanted to send at least one man back to justice. Kerle would die — on a rope.

There was some total satisfaction in ramming fists at the man's ugly face. And a quick twist disposed of the rifle and it was flung to one side. Then they were slugging bunched fists at each other again, two men filled with a savage need to beat the other to pulp.

Jim Gallery could have ended the whole thing right there by just whipping out his handgun and firing into Max Kerle. Instead, he had this deep down gutsy desire to hammer physically at the other man. And another fact — he wanted to take him back to legal justice.

But it was a mistake. Kerle seemed possessed by a vicious new sense of survival. Weaponless, he fought and kicked. His hands clawed momentarily at Jim Gallery's face; digging in a few fearful moments at Jim's very eyeball sockets. Jim rammed him back and the fingers scraped down his face, taking blood and skin.

Sucking for breath, the two men backed from each other for about ten seconds.

'I knew you were there, Kerle,' breathed Jim Gallery. 'I had this sixth sense — and I heard a click — a metallic click. It was you, Kerle, trying the rifle action. It was a good thing for me there was a loose plank on the other side of this cabin.'

Max Kerle's reply was a kick that nearly broke Jim's right leg. The boot connected with damnable speed. The mistake in talking, in not killing this man began to show.

Jim's leg buckled. He stumbled to one side. Kearle hit him again, a real thump that would have dazed even a prizefighter. Jim Gallery teetered, gasping, trying to gain time, sure that he could still best this man and take him prisoner.

At that moment Delia Breen chose to open the shack door and dart into the night. Fast as a rattler striking back, Max Kerle saw his chance. He stepped back and grabbed at the girl and held her like a shield before him. In his terrific grip she did not stand a chance of escape.

Max Kerle had seen the Colt in Jim's holster; had figured it was only a matter of time before the fisticuffs ended with a gun blasting at him. The girl was his only chance.

He backed away, dragging the girl with him. In that moment Jim Gallery whipped out his handgun — and hesitated, cursing. Every passing second was another yard of getaway for Max Kerle. He knew the big horse that had belonged to Stephen Crane was right behind him — and that was the animal with the gold bags. Sure, he was weaponless — but if he could only get away, beat the threat of the other man's gun, he had a chance.

Twice Jim Gallery aimed the Colt and trembled on the point of firing, but every moment was one in which the girl and the man jerked and twisted. It was impossible to shoot without the risk of hitting the girl.

Max Kerle reached the horse, laughed jeeringly, the girl still like a living shield. He knew he had a problem. He wasn't away yet. He still had to hit the saddle.

Out of a lifetime of dirty rough-house tricks came the answer. Gallery had a gun; he had the girl. Gallery would not risk her death. And death could come to this girl if he wished it because he knew how to kill her before the very eyes of the man with the gun.

Jim Gallery trembled with fury and inner reproaches for having fooled with this ruffian. He had yielded to other considerations. They were rapidly looking like mistakes. Unless Kerle slipped up and offered a chunk of his anatomy as a target.

But the hardcase was close to the horse — the animal with the gold bags still tied to the saddle pommel, Jim noted — and the girl kicking and struggling in his unrelenting grip. Kerle slid a thick arm around her neck, cutting off her screams.

'Listen, Gallery — drop your gun. Yes — drop it — because if you don't I'm gonna break the neck of this little beauty right before your eyes.'

The way he held the girl proved it was no idle threat. His arm was around her neck so tightly that Delia Breen's screams suddenly rasped into an ugly choking sound. Jim Gallery swallowed rage and disappointment like bad medicine. But he still held the gun. Instinctively, it still pointed at the struggling pair.

'I mean it, Gallery,' the other man raged. 'I'll break her neck, so help me! You want that?'

'I'd still kill you.'

'The girl would be dead. I ask you

again — d'you want that?' Jim Gallery saw the horror in the girl's eyes as her neck was forced back, slowly, remorselessly, by the ruthless arm that held her. Shocked, he knew there was a time element of only seconds in which to decide.

Jim Gallery's gun dropped to the ground. 'Let her go — now!'

Still mentally as alert as a savage Indian, Max Kerle knew all his next actions would have to be thrust into seconds of swift movement.

He pushed the girl from him like a sack thrown from a train and at the same time he leaped to the saddle of the big horse.

He dug heels at the animal's flanks with complete cruelty and the mount sprang forward with coiled haunches.

Jim Gallery was, of necessity, moments behind all this play and although he dived like a madman for his Colt again, there was only a disappearing shade in the night at which to pump off some desperate shots. The gun roared and the slugs cut the night air, but the whole circle of movement was too fast for accuracy. And with the luck of his breed, Max Kerle flattened on the saddle and tore into the darkness.

The girl sprawled motionless. Jim cursed his indecision. He hated to feel he had been bested. Even at that moment Kerle had him hogtied. The girl looked in a bad way; he couldn't go off on the other horse in pursuit of Kerle and leave her.

He crouched over her, brought her around by holding her and gently slapping her cheek.

Delia Breen fluttered her eyelids and, for a moment, looked fearfully into his face.

'You'll be all right,' he muttered. 'He's gone.'

'Please get me away from here,' she entreated. 'This hateful shack . . . and that dead man . . . I just want to get away.'

'We'll be riding out,' he agreed.

'We've got mounts. We'll get back to town.' He stared again at the silent, dark land beyond them. There was something mocking about the way the night had helped Kerle. The man was out there, covering distance and no doubt gloating.

'I'll get you into town and safety then — ' He did not finish his sentence but he knew with a sense of finality what his next action would be. He'd go after Max Kerle. He would, after all, kill the man — and retrieve that gold.

He had horses to round up and one body to tie over a saddle. He found Max Kerle's mount out in the night after some searching and making sympathetic noises. He needed the animal for Stephen Crane's body. The big man would travel back to town the undignified way.

There were so many things to do; the journey back and explanations to Helen Mackay and the deputy in Delta. He felt tired of it all. Only the thought of meeting Helen cheered him.

When they were ready to go, the girl glanced back at the old shack. 'Hateful! How can I ever forget . . . that man . . . ?'

'You will,' mumbled Jim Gallery. 'You're just a kid, Delia. You'll forget.'

They rode back down the trail, bound for Delta and the comfort of bed and food.

When they finally entered Delta it was getting late but more important than that fact was Helen Mackay's reaction when she saw him.

'You're in a terrible mess! Look at you — blood and dust all over your face.' She clutched his shirtsleeve. 'Now where do you think you're going?'

'After Kerle. He's got your gold . . . '

She gasped. 'At this time of the night — and the physical state you're in! Oh, Jim — give up. It doesn't matter about the gold.'

'It sure does — to me,' he muttered. 'And being bested matters.'

Her brown eyes swept him. 'You look

all in. You need rest and food. Who do you think you are? You can't ride all night. You'll fall off that darned horse with fatigue . . . '

Grinning faintly at her slightly bossy tone, he allowed himself to be taken in hand. He needed food — that was true. He needed some attention given to the gouged cuts on his face. And he knew in his heart that even Max Kerle would not ride all night. He'd hole up somewhere.

The deputy gave him a bunk in one of the cells, with extra blankets to show that this was preferential treatment. He heard Jim's story about Stephen Crane. 'He's wanted. You'll check on that. He and his pals killed the sheriff. That's enough to indict him — but there's plenty more.'

The deputy nodded, his narrowed eyes resting suspiciously on Jim Gallery's battered face and dirty clothing. 'And you, mister? You don't talk a lot about yourself. Who are you? Where d'you come from?'

'Just passing by,' returned Jim Gallery. 'You need to know no more than that.'

The man shut up, wisely deciding to make inquiries later. Jim finished his grub and rolled up in his blankets. He slept because he was bone weary but with a head filled with madly swirling thoughts, it wasn't the best kind of sleep.

He was up when the first light filtered into the cell. Walking stiffly, he went to a mirror. He decided he'd clean up, eat again and then get a fresh horse from some livery. He was going after Max Kerle — and nobody was going to stop him.

Helen Mackay guessed he was itching to push on and she left her friend's house very early and intercepted Jim Gallery as he adjusted the cinch on a horse outside the sheriff's office. She noted his cleaned-up face — but thought that his clothes were still a mess! She saw the gun in his holster and the rifle he had borrowed from the deputy.

'Jim, we don't need the gold . . . '

'You and your father worked damned hard for it,' he grunted. His eyes flashed. 'Why should a louse like Kerle grab it? You asking me to accept that?'

'You want to kill him,' she accused.

'He bested me . . . '

'But killing?'

'D'you think I can rest when all I can see in the back of my mind is that taunting devil?' he said in a sudden rage. 'No, Helen, I've just got to go after him.'

There was also Harry Carslake, who still rode high and wide. Would he hunt him down also? The man had the loot from the Drago Cattlemen's Bank and he had killed and double-crossed in order to get it. Was it worth hunting? Looking for Harry Carslake meant going back to the killer trail; meant identifying himself with guns and death. Would he do that? Or would the trail end with Max Kerle?

He said nothing to the girl about

these thoughts. Anyway, he was unresolved about Harry Carslake — but Kerle and the gold would be tracked. And then, maybe, he'd consider Harry Carslake.

Helen glanced again at the saddle-scabbard and the Colt in his holster. 'Guns. I always seem to see you with guns . . . '

Something made him take her arm tenderly. 'I can live without them. I'll be back, Helen — and you'll see. Now I'm goin'. That deputy seems mighty anxious to keep track of me. I'm riding out before he figures to come along with me.'

He rode fast out of Delta, the horse fresh, the watery sun on his back. The grassy slopes just out of the town still held the morning dew. Dust kicked up beneath the flying hoofs.

Miles out, near a spread, he saw cowpokes chasing some cattle and, momentarily, envied their settled existence.

He had a pretty shrewd idea where

Max Kerle would head. Gold was something that most men like Kerle would want to turn into cash at the first opportunity. They could have done that in Delta — Crane, Dawson and Kerle — but that chance was gone and two were dead. So it was a pretty good guess that Max Kerle would head for Salida.

Jim Gallery drew an imaginary line in his mind from the old mission where Crane had died to the direction of Salida, and he figured he would get to that line after an hour of fast riding.

After that, hell only knew how, when or where he'd meet up with Kerle.

As he rode, urging the willing horse on, he got the fixation in mind like a burr sticking to his vest; he'd get the gold back for Helen and her father; that was his reason for pursuing Max Kerle.

And if the man got killed, that was tough luck.

But his whole line of thinking got a severe jolt when his horse went swiftly up a ridge and, poised, he found himself staring into a small valley. There was a horse, lying dead, an ugly shape on the grass and sand, and the colour of the animal's hide jogged his memory. It was the mount that Max Kerle had taken. Dead? What had happened? Where was Kerle? And then, staring, he saw the small, neat house only half a mile away, at the end of the grassy valley. Smoke curled from a stone chimney.

12

The Last Shot

Jim Gallery crouched over the dead horse. He noted at once that the big animal had broken a leg. And someone had put a slug into the big head, no doubt to end the creature's misery.

That brought him up sharply, thinking. He remembered that Max Kerle had been gunless when he had ridden out into the night. The man had lost his rifle when it had been wrested from his grasp. And he had no handgun. But someone had shot this animal.

There was no doubt that this was the horse that Max Kerle had used to get away from the old shack near the mission. And the saddle, and other gear were missing. Naturally, there was no sign of the gold.

Once again, Jim Gallery stared at the

little house in the distance. On further scrutiny he knew the place belonged to some homesteader; the tended fields around the stone and timber building were evidence of hard work by someone. He heard some hens cackling; the sound of some cows in a barn. The smoke from the chimney signified people. Was Max Kerle one of them? Or had he bought or stolen a horse and taken off?

Jim vaulted to his saddle again and went on, his hat pulled low over his eyes.

When he got really close and could see the clean, chintz drapes at the small windows, the door opened and a girl stepped out.

She held a shotgun in her two hands. Her face was pale and set. She pointed the gun at Jim Gallery and he halted his horse. 'This is as far as you go, mister. What do you want?'

His lips twisted in a quizzical smile and he drawled, 'Just passing, ma'am. I mean no harm. Tell me, have you seen that dead horse out there?'

'I have. Why — why — do you ask?'

He paused before replying, taking a lot of time, staring at the shotgun and seeing a great deal more. The girl was young, her straw-coloured hair twisted into a bun at the back of her head and she wore a cheap gingham dress. He noticed the plain wedding ring on her finger and wondered where her husband was. She was an attractive young woman, lithe-bodied and with some freckles. As he stared, drawing out the time, he noticed her apprehension and he was sure he wasn't causing it. So he smiled back.

'Broke a leg,' he said casually. 'Did you shoot it?'

She hesitated. Then, 'Er — yes — yes.'

'One of your horses, is it?'

'Yes. Go away. Ride on, mister. We've had trouble with — with — drifters before.'

'I ain't no drifter. Leastways, not the troublesome sort.' He tipped his hat.

'You got some water nearby, ma'am?'

'There's a well back of the house.'

Jim Gallery wheeled his mount; walked it around the gable-end of the house. He saw the well, went to it and cranked the bucket up. He let the horse drink and he slopped some water over his own face. All this casual activity took up some time and he was more than sure the girl was not alone.

She had gone inside the house when he rode around to the front again. He rode the horse out to a rocky bluff where the valley turned and that was the end of his retreat. He sat hunched in the saddle and pondered — and he was pretty sure the girl had been forced out to make a show with that scattergun.

Kerle. It was a fact that the dead horse had been his mount. The girl had lied about that. And quite likely she had not shot it — but she could have made a gun available to Max Kerle. Under some compulsion? Where was her husband?

Jim Gallery had a feeling of grim certainty that he need ride no further in his sombre search for Max Kerle. The man had holed-up in that homestead. His reasons were not so obvious. A picture of the slender, fair-haired girl came to him again and with it a hunch that women — like gold — were a lure to good and evil men alike.

He would play a waiting game, but what was happening inside that outwardly peaceful house? He didn't intend to wait until it was dark in order to learn the truth.

The house fronted mainly to the wide valley, but behind the place he had noticed the rising mounds of yellow dirt, the gullies and broken areas of land. That was the best way to approach the house. If he went back across the valley, they'd see him for a mile.

He edged the horse out of the hiding-place; went right down the valley, knowing he could not be seen behind the rocks and then came back through a number of gullies barely high enough to hide him. Soon he was behind the homestead, as near as he'd ever get and still stay in cover. He hitched the horse securely to a tough root that grew out of the side of the gully.

There was no hesitation, no hanging back. He had to go on, discover if his theories were sound, and the best way was the fast way.

There was open ground between him and the house; a kind of grassy waste which was yellowed with too much sun. He had to cross it. He knew he could be seen. But if he went as fast as an indian approaching a target, he might succeed.

He leaped forward, feet silent as possible and, crouching, went ahead in a swift race to the side of the house. It was a good hundred-yard sprint and he made it without inviting a gunshot or any other sign that he had been seen. He waited, drawing quick breaths. He listened, searching for a clue as to the occupants of the place. He had seen the girl — he thought Kerle might be inside — but was that all?

And then as if a signal to his probing mind, a shrill scream came from inside the house. The sound came from a feminine throat — and then there was a torrent of sobs and protests.

'No! No! Leave me alone! Oh — no — please — please!'

His face harsh, Jim Gallery raced to the door, darting along the blank gable-end. Hunches based on a number of sticky situations that had been his experience in the past told him that this was the time, to burst in, when some uncontrollable activity was going on.

Gun in hand, he rammed against the main door to the house and found it was not locked. He went in like some minor tornado and halted when he found himself in a big livingroom. And right there he froze.

'Hold it, Gallery!' came Max Kerle's ugly voice. 'You can drop that damned gun for a start.'

There was every reason to obey. Jim

took it all in like a flash. Kerle was holding the girl easily, although she was a spirited and strong creature, and he was also pointing a gun at the head of a man lying on a couch.

'You don't damned well give up!' snarled the gangling, hawklike man. 'I'm sick to hell of you, Gallery. Drop that gun — or I'll blast this feller's brains out on that couch.'

It was another rotten setup that seemed to be a special trick of Kerle's. Jim Gallery nearly triggered in sheer desperation — but every nerve in his head shrieked a warning that he could easily kill or wound the girl. Max Kerle held her, just as he had held Delia Breen the other night, and the girl did not keep still. She was jerking, twisting, really afraid and not in control of herself. Her dress was torn and pale skin showed near her breasts.

'I'll kill this feller if you fool around any more, Gallery!' The warning was savage, thick with hate and murderous intent. There was no doubt that Max

Kerle would kill.

Jim Gallery dropped his gun; saw it hit the floor with a kind of bitterness that nearly choked him.

'Better,' sneered Kerle. 'Now ain't this cosy? We might be able to relax. Until I get organized. Now — I take it you got a horse somewhere Gallery . . .'

'What's wrong with him?' Jim pointed at the man on the couch.

'He's my husband,' gasped the girl. 'He's ill — some sort of fever — I don't know what it is — but I've been nursing him.'

'Pretty little nurse, ain't she?' Max Kerle held her in a strong and insolent manner, his hand clamped close to her breast. 'I've been hangin' around hoping she'll be nice to me — but it seems I got to take everythin' I want in this life.'

'Let her go, man.'

'You kiddin'? Ain't she pretty? And all alone — at least she was until you showed up, Gallery — if you don't count her man, and he's real bad. He can't lift a finger . . . '

'You lost your horse?' Jim figured to ask questions; play for time.

'Broke a damn leg, the stupid nag . . . '

'You shot it? You should have dragged it away somewhere and I'd never have noticed it and probably would've ridden by.'

'Does it matter?' Max Kerle looked the epitome of evil intent, with his unshaven face and wild hair. His clothes were torn and filthy, the result of fights and hard-riding. In fact, the man hardly looked human. Distastefully watching him, Jim Gallery wondered fleetingly if this was the end result of the owlhoot trail for a man. Was it possible for any man to become such a stringy, smelling scarecrow?

Max Kerle waved his gun. 'Move over, Gallery. Get away from that gun. Hell, I could shoot you — right now — couldn't I? Ain't that something! I got you dead to rights, Gallery.'

'You got me,' agreed the other. Then, swiftly, in case the casual remark was inviting trouble, 'You've still got the gold, Kerle?'

The other man indulged in a raucous laugh. 'Stashed right here — in this house. I got all the aces.' Some need for satisfaction stalled Kerle's finger on the trigger. He eyed Jim Gallery as he held the girl masterfully in spite of her struggles. There was curiosity, a sort of speculation in Max Kerle's glittering eyes, showing that he knew Jim was at his mercy. 'You'll die here, Gallery, you know that. I've just got to squeeze this trigger . . . queer, ain't it? I mean, you and me . . . all we done together . . . with that blamed sarcastic Crane *hombre* deader than hell now . . . and Kid Dawson buzzard meat . . . just leaves me in one piece out of all that helling around . . . '

'Fate is pretty strange,' admitted Jim. He watched the girl jerk again; wondering how long the man would hold her; how long the talking spasm would last.

'You've tried to kill me.' Rage began to edge into Kerle's voice. 'More'n once . . . so it's right for you to die, Gallery. Wish to hell I could make it slow . . . ever seen a man pegged out with a hot fire burning into his chest? That's Injun style . . . pity I can't hand it out to you . . . '

The young wife began a fresh burst of resistance. A new fury drove her on, it seemed. But Max Kerle spent a full two minutes just beating down her strength with an arm that was like a band of steel. His gun in his right hand never wavered from Jim Gallery's body.

'You will pay in the end, my pretty,' Kerle grated a warning. 'I'm goin' to have you. Been a long time since I been with a gal as fresh as you. You'll lie with me, my lovely — unless you want that sick husband of yours to get his comeuppance. Surely you'd do that for him?' And Kerle laughed at his joke.

She became strangely quiet; lay in his

arms, her breasts rising and falling with her exertions. She glanced at Jim Gallery, as he stood tautly, hands upraised enough to placate Kerle. Then she looked full into the unwashed and unlovely face of Max Kerle. Eyes wide, fear making her skin clear and taut, she seemed to come to some terrible decision.

'I'll — I'll come with you — now — if you promise to leave my husband alone. Promise not to harm him — please . . . '

Kerle's laugh was thick with triumph. 'Wow! I'll treat you right, my beauty! Max will show you . . . '

She slid from his arm as his grip slackened slightly. He held her hand, not entirely allowing her to go. She paused, looked at him with all the temptation that a woman can reveal on her face and with her free hand she slid the torn dress down near one breast.

An ugly sound escaped Max Kerle's throat. 'By hell, you're for me, woman! And you — Gallery — you're dead!'

'Let him go,' breathed the girl. 'Please let him go.'

Max Kerle levelled his gun. 'Not a chance. I hate his blasted guts. He's bested me . . . tried to kill me . . . I tell you — he's goin' to die!'

The girl was still dragging her hand from Max Kerle's grip. She was moving to a door on the other side of the room which, it seemed, was a bedroom. Jim Gallery watched with a fixed scowl, wondering about his chances of jumping Max Kerle. But the man kept at a distance although he moved a few slow, edging steps with the girl. The man on the couch gave a sudden moan and writhed as some fever wracked him.

'I don't want killin' in this house,' pleaded the girl. She moved again. Her hand was still gripped by the dirty paw of the ruffian and he moved with the girl. Then with a taunting smile that only gave his face an uglier appearance, he halted.

'I'll blast this hellion,' he snapped, 'and then we'll be together, my pretty.

You won't regret it. I reckon I need you — and I'll not touch a hair of your goddamn hubby's head . . . '

Max Kerle half-turned, began to level the gun with the appearance of finality. The girl was at least two steps away from him, her eyes fixed on the unkempt man. Kerle had released her hand.

Jim Gallery knew the end was pretty well nigh to hand. If he hesitated another second a slug would tear into his flesh and Kerle would not err in this final, vicious, accurate shooting.

Knowing it was a desperate try with only a marginal chance of success, he dived for Kerle's boots with all the crashing speed he could muster. His breath rasped into a hoarse cry as he plumetted like a jet for the filth-encrusted boots. Even as he shot like some projectile, despair filled him, knowing he had no chance, that a shot would crash out at any split-second and rip the life out of him.

He touched the man's feet, clawed

— and then the shot roared out in the confined space of the homestead livingroom.

A man's yell of agony seared the graceful room and echoed like the dying howl of some animal.

Jim Gallery rolled, fast wits telling him in a shattered moment that something had happened; that he had a chance to live.

He tumbled like an acrobat across the floor, almost frenzied as he turned on his hands and knees to glance at the scene.

The girl had a gun in her hand and smoke still wisped from the barrel. Jim recognized it in a flash; his gun! The one he had dropped at Kerle's command.

As for Max Kerle, he was on his knees, his face twisting in pain, his eyes shining with the horror of approaching death. Blood already stained a patch on his shirt, right over his heart, mixing with the dirt that seemed to be his trademark.

The young wife stared, slowly lowering the handgun. Jim Gallery jumped to his feet; went over and gently took the instrument of death from her. She glanced at him, her face breaking into sudden tremulous movements as the whole reaction flooded every nerve in her being.

'I had to do it.' She breathed the statement. 'That animal — he would have defiled me. I — I — wouldn't have given myself to him . . . '

'I know,' said Jim Gallery gently.

'I just figured — if only I could get that gun — so I had to play him along — I — I — fooled him, didn't I?'

Jim stared at Max Kerle as the man finally toppled forward and died. His body became a lifeless hulk which dripped blood.

'You saved my life,' said Jim. 'And you rid the world of this man. I'm glad of that. You saved me the job.'

The girl clutched at a chair and sat down. She tried to pull her torn dress together. 'Who is he? Not that it matters . . . he's dead . . . isn't he?'

'Ready for the mortuary,' said Jim Gallery. 'And don't worry about who he is — or was. He was just one of the killer stamp.'

'He — he came here early this morning — full of some plausible tale — and borrowed a gun to kill the horse — and then he started to show his awful intentions the moment he got back to this house. I stalled him — for a long time — pleaded with him — he seemed to enjoy making me squirm — and then you showed up. He forced me to go out with the shotgun — '

'You don't need to tell me any more.' Jim Gallery holstered his gun. 'I'll help you clean up; get this skunk out of your nice house. He's goin' back to Delta — to Boothill. And I'll see about a doctor for your husband, ma'am.'

Jim found the gold. The girl showed him where Kerle had stashed it. He sat down and looked at the little sacks of the heavy metal, hard lines etching his face at his multitude of thoughts.

There was still Harry Carslake. One man who rode free and laughed at him; one man who relied on a fast horse and guns to keep all the advantages of the loot from the Drago Cattlemen's Bank.

Jim hauled Kerle's body out onto the hardbaked ground outside the house. He went back and cleaned up for the girl as promised. She was bending over her husband, wiping his face with a damp cloth.

'I'll get my horse and then I'll go, ma'am,' he said. 'And let me say — thanks for saving my life.'

'You saved me,' she said quietly, 'by just turning up.'

As he rode back down the valley, the unlovely body tied to the back of his saddle, he thought again of Harry Carslake. There was only one answer; the hell with him! He'd had enough of the vengeance trail. Let Harry Carslake ride and spend his life looking back for a pursuer.

In Delta, he found Helen again. She was with the deputy in the sheriff's office, and she ran to Jim Gallery, the moment she saw him. She threw her arms around him, unashamedly, hugging this tall, grim-faced man in the travel-stained clothes.

'Oh, you're safe. Thank goodness!'

The deputy eyed the body on the horse. 'Another?'

'A killer who's quit killin' . . . '

'I'll get him over to the mortuary,' sighed the lawman. 'You can tell me the tale — but I think I know enough.'

'Good,' said Jim Gallery, 'because I want to talk to this lady.' He took Helen to a quiet corner of the boardwalk and placed an arm around her shoulders. 'It's all over. I mean the shooting. There's going to be no more — if I can help it. And I want to tell you all about myself . . . '

She searched his face, smiled shyly. 'I think I know enough about you — but tell me as much as you want if it will do any good. One thing I know — you're a real man. You fight for rough justice.'

He nodded with some finality. 'Guns

and justice. Oh, let's forget all that stuff. I'm cleaning up — and taking you to some nice place where a man and a girl can eat and talk — about the future. That's important — our future.'

THE END